Growing Wings

Growing Wings

by
Laurel Winter

sandpiper

Houghton Mifflin Harcourt
Boston   New York

The Library of Congress has cataloged the hardcover edition as follows:

Winter, Laurel.
Growing wings / Laurel Winter. p. cm.
Summary: When wings start to appear on her back, eleven-year-old Linnet begins
to understand some of her mother's strange behavior, but it isn't until she finds
herself at a remote house in Montana with others who also have—or had—wings
that she can really come to terms with her situation.

ISBN 978-0-618-07405-1
ISBN 978-0-547-24904-9 pa
[1. Wings—Fiction. 2. Curiosities and wonders—Fiction.
3. Self-acceptance—Fiction.] 1. Title.
PZ7.W757 Gr 2000
[Fic]—dc21
00-027584

Manufactured in the United States of America

EB 10 9 8 7 6 5 4 3 2 1

ACKNOWLEDGMENTS

First of all, I want to thank my parents, Johnny and Donna Hjelvik, for raising me in the mountains of Montana and letting me buy all the books I wanted from the school book clubs, since the nearest library was so far away. Like them, my husband, Bruce Winter, and my sons, Nick and Zach, have been supportive of all my creative pursuits—and that is valuable beyond belief. This is true for my in-laws, Mal and Beth Winter, as well.

Next, thanks to the members of various fiction critique/support groups: Selby Beeler, Catherine Friend, Heidi Magnuson, Eleanor Arnason, Terry A. Garey, Eric M. Heideman, Phillip C. Jennings, Lyda Morehouse, John Calvin Rezmerski, Marcella Chester, Winnie Donoghue, Cheryl Finnegan, Debbie Hill Fuehrer, Coralee Grebe, Laurie Neubecker Lanzdorf, Bob Luck, Cathy Nagler, Laurel Panser, Cathy Tacinelli, Gary Wick, Linda Essig, C. J. Fosdick, and Linda Kolter. And, since all writing is related, *merci beaucoups* to the members of my poetry groups: Root River Poets, The Ladies' Tea & Poetry Salon, and Group of 8. My husband, Bruce, helped me with the photography sections, and Almae Larson gave me further input. My art teacher, Sally Brown, helped me realize how interconnected all of my creativity is.

Fandom—that strange and wonderful subculture found at science fiction conventions—is an incredible gift to readers and writers of science fiction and fantasy.

Several professional groups also have helped me: the Science Fiction and Fantasy Writers of America (SFWA), the Society of Children's Book Writers and Illustrators (SCBWI), the League of Minnesota Poets, the National Federation of State Poetry Societies, the National Writers' Union, and Toastmasters International.

Last in the chain of events leading to the publication of this book—but perhaps most important—are the great people at Houghton Mifflin: my editor, Ann Rider; associate editor Kim Keller; art director Bob Kosturko; and all the others whose names I don't yet know.

This list is incomplete. I have so many terrific friends, relatives, and colleagues who have helped me fly—Tracey, Shelly, Mikol, Janet Munger, Uncle Dave—but I have to stop lest the list be longer than the book. Thanks to all of you.

Laurel Winter
January 2000

To everyone who has ever dreamed of flying.
And to everyone who dares to grow wings.

CHAPTER

One

Linnet waited with her eyes closed for the door to open and her mother to peek in. Waited for her to touch Linnet's shoulder blades lightly and pull the covers up and go. Linnet knew that touch in her bones, as if it had happened every night of her life, even when she had been sleeping. An imprint, a memory of the skin itself. Not like a caress— more like a nurse taking a pulse or checking for swelling.

It made no sense. But then, so many things about her mother made no sense. Like why she told the school Linnet had a heart murmur, when she really didn't. Like why she wouldn't let Linnet cut her hair. Like why she would never talk about any relatives, including Linnet's father. Like—

The itching interrupted her thoughts. Linnet grabbed her hair and twisted it out of the way, reaching back with her left hand and scratching one shoulder, then the other. Something was wrong with her. Beneath the itch was an ache. And there were weird bumps on both shoulders.

Her mother's light footsteps. Linnet almost missed them. She stilled her movement just as the door opened, leaving her hand flopped back over her right shoulder, as if she had fallen asleep in that position.

Her mother's gentle fingers. Her gasp, so light Linnet could barely hear. She reached out and grabbed her mother's hand. "What's the matter with me?" she cried. "Do I have cancer? What's wrong?"

Her mother bowed her head in the darkness and wept, cupping the two itchy places on Linnet's back with hands as small as those of a child. Linnet, too, was tiny. At eleven, she was as small as an eight-year-old.

The words ran together. "I'm so sorry, I wasn't sure." She caught Linnet into a fierce hug. "Oh, now what do we do, I won't do it, I won't." One hand tangled in Linnet's long hair; the other held her hard. "I'm sorry," she said again, her breath hot against Linnet's head. "But they'll see."

"See what?" asked Linnet, scared by her mother's tears, half-crying herself. "What's the matter with my back?"

"Wings—you're growing wings."

"Huh?" asked Linnet, even more bewildered than before. "Wings?" She felt numb, slow, dense. None of this made any sense.

"I was so afraid of this."

"Why did you think I was going to grow wings?" Linnet asked.

Her mother let go. She turned on the light. Her face looked pale, rimmed with a rainbow from the tears caught on Linnet's lashes as she squinted against the light.

Her mother began to unbutton her shirt. Linnet shrank into herself, more scared, smaller. She had never even seen her mother in a swimming suit. Some of her friends' mothers, but never her own. Something was very wrong.

The delicate fingers undid the buttons. Her mother turned around, so her back was to Linnet, and, head bowed, she slowly dropped her shirt.

Two scars bloomed like flowers on her back. Without knowing she was going to, Linnet reached out. Her mother flinched, and Linnet drew back. "No, it's okay." Her mother's voice was almost inaudible. "Go ahead. You can touch."

But Linnet didn't want to. "What were they?" she asked, even though she knew. Her voice shook. Her stomach felt sick. Her shoulders ached and itched.

Her mother pulled the shirt back over her shoulders and buttoned it before she turned around. She raised her chin. "Wings," she said.

Linnet just stared. "People don't get wings."

"When I was ten years old," said her mother, "my shoulder blades began to itch and ache." She sounded as if she were telling a tale she had practiced in her head but never

3

told anyone. "My mother wrapped a strip of cloth around and around me." She touched Linnet just above the place where her breasts would grow. "Here, and passing under my arms. Tight. So tight I thought I couldn't breathe. My back hurt. Every other day, my mother took off the cloth and made me take a bath. She wouldn't let me touch my back. After I was dry, she bound me up again."

Linnet just sat, her own back resting against the wall.

"This went on for weeks, months, over a year. And then one night the phone rang just as I was getting out of the bath. My mother went to answer it..."

Sarah McKenzie's eyes were clouded with pain. "I took a hand mirror and looked at the reflection of my back in the mirror over the sink. Wings—squashed and twisted and flattened by the binding. But wings." She reached one hand over her shoulder, as if she still felt them there. "And then my mother came back into the bathroom and found me looking at them. She screamed and broke the mirrors and made me promise never to tell anyone and never to touch them. And I never did." Her hand dropped.

"But your back..." said Linnet.

"When I was almost twelve," said Sarah, her voice hardening, "my mother decided that even binding couldn't hide them anymore. She fed me as much brandy as I could drink, tied me to the table, and cut off my wings. I almost died. When I was fifteen, I ran away."

"But why didn't you get wings when you were little?" Linnet asked, meaning also *Why am I getting them now?*

Her mother's face turned red. "I think it has something to do with puberty," she said.

Linnet wanted to squirm. Here she was, this little shrimpy kid who looked as if she were in third grade, chest as flat as a field, and she was about to start her period. And grow wings. She flopped down on her pillow and sobbed.

Gentle hands caressed her back. "You need some time to yourself," said Sarah. "Call if you need me."

The door closed behind her, and Linnet was alone in the dark, with wing bumps on her shoulders. This was why her mother had given her the name of a bird. And this was why she had never seen her mother's back, even in a bathing suit or sundress. She could see the scars in the air before her, even when she closed her eyes.

She did not sleep soon or well.

Dreams of bleeding from her shoulders, having her hands bound, hearing her mother scream as great, feathered wings were ripped from her shoulders—

"Stop, stop, stop." It was her mother's voice. She gripped Linnet's hands tightly; there was blood on Linnet's fingers. "You have to stop—you'll hurt yourself."

Linnet wakened the rest of the way. The deep, maddening itch was still there, but it was accompanied by stinging pain.

"You were scratching yourself." Sarah cautiously released Linnet's hands.

"I can't stand it," said Linnet, working her shoulders up and down against the sheets.

"You can," Sarah said flatly. "I'll help, but you can."

Linnet thought of her mother as a child, what she had withstood: the binding cloth, the brandy and the knife. "Okay," she said.

Sarah sprinkled uncooked oatmeal into a deep, warm bath. "I'm not sure how much this will help, but stay in as long as you like."

"But school—"

"I'll take you later, if you feel like going. Just call me at work and I'll come get you. Copies R Us will survive for half an hour without me."

After her mother left the room, Linnet slipped out of her nightshirt and lowered herself into the water. It stung for a second, but then it was better, much better. She settled in deeper, with just her face and knees above the surface. What kind of bird was she, anyway, that she liked water? A penguin was the first bird that came to mind. She sat up rather fast.

"Mother," she yelled in the direction of the closed bathroom door. "Mother!"

Sarah stuck her head in. "Does it help? What do you need?"

"It's great," said Linnet, shrugging off the questions.

"Can I fly? If my wings grow out? Or will they be like penguin wings?"

There was a silence, and then her mother's bitter voice. "How would I know?"

"Maybe your mother knows," said Linnet, without thinking.

Sarah flung the door open. A wave of cold air hit Linnet. "I have not seen that woman for thirteen years. I hope she's dead."

Linnet sank back down into the warmth. "I'm sorry. I'm sorry."

"So am I."

It wasn't until Linnet peeked up again, over the edge of the tub, that she knew the door was closed and her mother was gone.

As the water cooled, thoughts flooded through her. She was growing wings. Maybe she was an alien. Could she be from another planet, where everyone had wings and they flew through a weird-colored sky? Or could she be some sort of mutant, like the three-legged frogs they'd studied in science, changed by pollution or radiation or something? Wings.

Linnet turned on the faucet, scooting her feet out of the way and swishing the hot currents toward the back of the tub until the water level reached the overflow drain and started gurgling out. She slowly lay back, submerging until only the tiniest oval of her face was exposed to the air.

A shiver ran through her. Perhaps someday she would be able to fly. There could be no other reason for having wings, could there? The unbidden images of ostriches and penguins popped up again, and she shoved them aside.

She felt her face settle into a stubborn expression. One thing was for sure: she was not going to let anyone bind her wings or cut them off.

The note she took to school was simple: "Please excuse Linnet from the first two periods. She wasn't feeling well. Sarah McKenzie." Linnet was grateful for her long, wavy hair, which made a curtain over her back; she wished it covered her face as well. Would the wings have feathers? She would have to ask her mother. Perhaps that was a safe question.

"What was the problem, Linnet?" asked the school secretary, taking the note in her efficient fingers.

"I just didn't feel well." They had discussed what to say and thought it would be better not to settle on a specific area that might then be examined by the school nurse.

"You didn't have a fever, did you?" The secretary's voice sharpened. It was against policy to come to school within twenty-four hours of having a fever.

"No," said Linnet.

"Well, you certainly are pale." The secretary looked her over, apparently made a decision, and impaled the excuse on a metal spike. "You're too late for the hot lunch count. Did you bring a cold lunch?"

"I had a late breakfast," said Linnet. Miraculously, this was her first lie of the conversation.

"Go ahead and go to class, then."

It was impossible to keep from scratching. Linnet caught herself doing it again and again. Others caught her, too, both students and teachers. "Linnet's got cooties," she heard one boy say, which caused a general laugh.

"If she does, she caught them from you," Roxie said back. Roxie was the closest Linnet had to a best friend, which meant they hung around at school together sometimes, since Linnet's mother never let her have friends over. Plus Roxie was always busy with soccer or gymnastics or something, and she tended to hang out with the rest of the jocks most of the time. She and Linnet didn't actually have much in common, but she was friendlier than most of the kids. Still, she wasn't the type of person that Linnet could tell about wings.

None of the grownups said anything, except the librarian, who rather liked Linnet and felt sorry for her because she had to stay in the media center rather than go to gym. That fictitious heart murmur! Now Linnet could understand why her mother had made it up. In middle school, she'd have to start using a locker room. If by any chance the wings were still a secret by then, the locker room would be the kiss of death.

The librarian leaned over her. "You are squirmy today, Linnet," she whispered. "Is something the matter?"

Linnet shrugged. "Not really," she said. Unless you count growing wings. "I guess I just . . . had too much sugar . . . for breakfast . . . on my cereal, I mean."

"Maybe you'd better have toast tomorrow—and skip the jelly."

Fortunately, with all the accusations of abuse around the country, there wasn't a teacher in the school who would touch a student, or Linnet would have received a pat on the shoulder right about then.

"Ms. Penn," she said, just before the librarian could turn away. "Are there any stories about people who can fly?"

The librarian scrunched up her face the way she always did when she was thinking. "We have some mythology books about Icarus. You know, the boy whose father made wings and—"

"No, I mean *people* with wings."

"How about angels? We might have something on angels."

She wasn't an angel. Was she? "No, not angels. People."

There wasn't anything, really, except for folktales and fiction and some stuff about levitation. Nothing about people with actual wings. Except, of course, for angels, and that seemed rather unlikely. Wouldn't a person know if she were an angel?

She tried a Web search, too. Plenty of stuff on airplanes and flying disks and hockey teams. Birds. Insects. Flying squirrels. Bats. She was about to give up when she saw a Web site called WingNet, about various myths of people with wings, including current urban myths. "Myths," she muttered. "Hah. I could tell them about their stupid myths." There was an e-mail address, and her fingers hovered over the keyboard for a second, but it made her uneasy to think of someone being able to find her. Then the bell rang for the next period, and Linnet quickly logged off so no one could tell what she had been searching for.

By the time the school day was over, the itching was unbearable. Or by the time the itching was unbearable, the school day was over. Linnet ran outside, hoping she'd see her mother's gray car so she wouldn't have to ride the bus through noisy, crowded stop after stop. She had to get home. She had to.

And she did, crying all the way in the passenger seat. "I can't—" she started to say once, but a glance at her mother's back stopped her short.

Wings. Forming beneath the surface of her skin. Unfolding. Emerging.

Once they were out, tiny and jointed, the itching stopped. Still, her fingers found their way to her back, exploring the topography of the small, growing protrusions.

The new, downy feathers were reddish brown, like the hair on her head, so the sight of them in the mirror was shocking.

But Linnet did like the feel of them—soft over strong. As for whether they would be big enough to allow her to fly, it was hard to say, but she thought maybe yes; they seemed to be growing every day.

She found it hard to imagine the twisted, stunted things they would become if they were bound like her mother's wings. Linnet felt waves of anger toward her unknown grandmother. How could she? And yet both she and her mother were beginning to understand, as the wings grew and strained against the fabric of Linnet's shirts. How could she not?

Sarah didn't look at Linnet's wings. Hardly ever talked anymore. When she didn't think Linnet was looking, she embraced herself, fingertips touching the horrible scars hidden beneath her blouse, and wept silently.

The assistant principal called Linnet into his office. Linnet sat very straight, not leaning against the back of the chair. She adjusted her hair and held her head still.

"Is something bothering you?"

"No," said Linnet. She never shrugged anymore; the wings were getting too big for her to do anything to call attention to her back.

"Everything's all right at home?" His voice was kind, but his eyes were clinical. Linnet knew that anything she said, and things she didn't say but he suspected, were going to be written down and put in her file.

"It's fine," she said.

"Your teachers tell me you seem upset a lot these days."

Linnet fought back a wave of sadness before it got to her eyes. "It's nothing," she said. "Really."

The assistant principal sighed. "Very well," he said. "If you ever need to talk to someone, though, you can come to me. Or to one of your teachers."

Sure, tell one of her teachers that she was growing wings covered with fine, auburn feathers. "Thank you," said Linnet. She rose carefully and backed out of the room. Soon, though, she wouldn't have to tell anyone, because the wings would be visible in spite of her long hair and loose clothes. It was a good thing school was almost out—one week to go. Then she could hide in the house for the summer. What would happen in the fall, though? She thought of her grandmother's knife and shuddered.

After supper, Linnet had taken to locking herself in her room with a stack of books. The public library had a lot of stuff about flying and wings—even if it didn't exactly apply to her situation. She read poetry, novels, nonfiction about the mechanics of flight, even picture books, searching for clues and comfort. If there were winged people in human history, she would find them.

By evening her wings ached from the confinement of her shirt, so she took it off and put on a bright green halter-top that did not interfere with the wings' movement. When she had first done this, the bare wings had made her feel self-conscious. Gradually, she had grown more used to them, although a sudden glance in the mirror still made her stomach lurch.

She was learning how to move her wings: how to spread them wide, how to fold them—although she didn't do this much in the evenings, since they'd been folded against her back for hours. And she was learning how to flap.

The first time she flapped her wings, she banged the tip of one painfully on the edge of her dresser and knocked a ceramic frog on the floor. One bulbous eye was chipped and two toes broken off.

Now she knew where to stand to flap safely—at the foot of the bed, holding on to the bedpost, with her back toward the locked door. Homework papers fluttered about as her wings disturbed the air. She ignored them, feeling fierce and wild and alone in the world.

Except she wasn't, couldn't be. There had to be others like her and her mother. There had to be someone who knew.

There has to be someone who knows. The thought would

not leave her. Someone knew whether winged people could fly. Someone knew why they had wings in the first place.

Linnet flapped more and more slowly until she was still, clinging to the bedpost, sweating with exertion and fear. Then she folded her wings and unlocked her door.

She had never bared her wings to her mother. She hesitated, a chick perched on the edge of a branch. Then she opened the door.

Birds migrate because they have to, not because they like to travel.

—*National Audubon Society*
First Field Guides: Birds

CHAPTER

Two

The color—what little there was—fled her mother's face. Linnet saw anger and jealousy and bitter sorrow and pride, all mixed together in an expression no face should wear. But no words. What words could say all those things her face was saying? Her face—and her hands, reaching back to her own shoulders, trying to see if there were still the seeds of wings at the roots of her scars.

"I have to know," said Linnet, her voice trying to be a whisper but coming out a demand. "I have to know if there's anyone else like me, or where we came from, or anything."

Still no words, still the emotions fighting on her mother's pale face. Finally, she nodded and covered her face with her own thin hands and wept.

Linnet lay awake that night, listening to the sounds of

her mother's weeping, stroking the tips of her wings, shuddering with fear and anticipation. Sometime after, she fell into sleep, fell into a dream where she was running from someone—she didn't know whom—and she came to a sharp cliff. The someone was coming closer, closer. She couldn't bear to be caught, so she leaped and fell, faster and faster, until she remembered to spread her wings, and then she was flying, soaring, spiraling with joy, and she hardly remembered that she'd been chased off the edge.

The day after school let out, Linnet awoke to a touch on the side of her face. "It's time to go." Without thinking, she stretched her wings, and her mother fled the room.

Linnet sat up. With the wings, she had switched to sleeping on her stomach, and she still wasn't used to it. She twisted her neck to get rid of a crick and looked around. It was a quarter to six. Her school backpack, which she hadn't worn the right way since the wings had emerged, was packed with clothes. Her most comfortable shirt and a pair of jeans were laid out on the end of the bed. How long had her mother been packing in the dimly lit room? Had she wanted to touch Linnet's wings?

Linnet grabbed the clothes and went into the bathroom. She peed, dressed, and struggled to pull a comb through her hair. It was just as well not to get it too smooth anyway; a web of tangles made a better shield for her shoulders.

When she went into the kitchen, her mother handed her a sandwich. Linnet wanted to ask a thousand questions, but she just accepted the sandwich—peanut butter, it looked like—and took her backpack out to the car.

By the time she had finished the sandwich, they were out of town. Linnet's mouth was dry from eating peanut butter plain: no butter, no jelly, nothing to drink. She wondered whether her mother had done it that way on purpose, to keep her from talking. She summoned up as much saliva as possible and rinsed it around.

Cars and seat belts are not designed for people with wings. Linnet sat twisted in the seat, facing the point where the steering column intersected the dash. She couldn't escape the sight of her mother's profile, which had settled into an expression that was no expression at all.

Maybe no expression was good, but Linnet hated it. She searched through the questions in her head for one guaranteed to provoke an expression. "Did my father have wings?"

Sarah turned her head and stared at Linnet longer than was comfortable, especially since she was driving the car. Now she just looked tired. "No," she said, focusing on the road again. "He had a charming, wicked smile and dark eyes, but no wings and no interest in any sort of permanent relationship." She paused for a moment, and her tiredness turned into the bitter look that seemed to occupy her face so often these days. "At least not with me. I only knew him for a month. By the time I found out I was pregnant, he'd taken off somewhere. I didn't even get the chance to decide if I was going to tell him about you or not."

That was not the story Linnet had imagined so many times in absence of the facts. In her version—versions, really, for she'd envisioned it several different ways—her father was someone who couldn't stay around and be with them. Like he was a spy, or someone in the witness protection program. Or he got amnesia and pretty soon he'd come out of it and remember and search them out. Or he was in prison, framed for a crime he didn't commit, and too ashamed to contact them until he was released. Not just someone who didn't care.

Linnet turned her head abruptly away, facing the side window.

"I'm sorry," Sarah said.

Linnet couldn't think of what to say, even if her throat would have let the words escape.

They were several days on the road. Seemed like months, years, centuries. Sarah's hands turned into bird claws, grasping the wheel. Linnet twisted all different directions, hard to do in a seat belt, trying to unscrunch her wings. They couldn't drive too far at a time.

Nights they spent at a Super 8 or Motel 6. Cheap. No pool, but then they couldn't have used one anyway. They developed a routine, without actually discussing it: after supper, Linnet would go to the room and lock herself in and let her wings free; Sarah would read magazines in the lobby or take a walk; when she knocked at the door, Linnet would cover up again and let her in.

The third night, Linnet lay on the bed, reading the comics and advice columns, flapping her wings in a lazy rhythm. She couldn't bear to let them be still in the short time available for movement. Sarah always came back before Linnet was ready to fold them against her back and cover them with a sweatshirt. They'd bought two extra-larges at a truck stop, one with loons and one proclaiming the mosquito as Minnesota's state bird. Linnet had made the joke only once, that *she* could be a state bird. Sarah hadn't laughed. Now they were in Livingston, Montana, with who-knew-what state bird.

Linnet finished the advice column and went on to the hints column, since her mother wasn't back yet. Some woman had written a tip on making little toilet paper cozies; she sounded so proud of herself. Linnet snorted and dropped the paper on the floor. She stretched her wings up and out, then beat them furiously for a few seconds. Still no mother.

She fell asleep waiting.

When she woke up, the other bed was still untouched. A hollowness opened in her, and fear flew wildly around within it.

Her mother didn't return all morning. Linnet sat in the

motel room and waited, not sure what to do. Surely she'd come back soon.

But she didn't.

It was stupid to just sit there, Linnet decided. She looked around the room for clues. The bed had not been slept in, but the bedspread was a little messed up near the nightstand, as if someone had been sitting there. There was a pad of paper on the nightstand, with nothing written on it. No help there. Linnet took a closer look. There were indentations in the blank page. Nothing she could read, though.

Linnet started to cry. The tissues in the bathroom were made of something that was clearly related to sandpaper. She grabbed one anyway and went back to the nightstand, wiping her eyes. She had to figure out what was written on that stupid notepad.

She dropped the tissue into the wastebasket and took another look. There were several crumpled pieces of notepaper in the bottom. "Oh, please," she whispered to herself, reaching in.

Notes from her mother. Started. Scratched out. Crumpled up. "Dear Linnet, I can't," something scribbled out that she couldn't read, "this is," end of note. The second one: "I'm going to"—check out? Hard to read, but maybe it was check out, then a bunch of scribbled stuff— "her house." Her grandmother's house?

Had her mother checked out of the motel? Maybe she

21

was supposed to go to her grandmother's house. The hollowness grew until it filled her. She felt light enough to fly with her fledgling wings, small enough to disappear—as her mother had disappeared.

But how was she supposed to find her grandmother's house?

The last scrunched note gave her a way to the answer. "Margaret McKenzie," it said, crossed out, but not completely obliterated. Linnet imagined her mother, sitting on the bed, watching her daughter sleep, writing these notes, changing her mind, crumpling them up. But why hadn't she left a real note?

There was a phone book in the drawer. Only one Margaret McKenzie listed. Linnet wrote down the address, her fingers shaking.

She stared at what she had written. When she reached the address, her mother would not be there waiting. Just some crazy old grandmother who might tie her up and cut off her wings. That was no good. Maybe her mother would come back.

There was no answer at their home number, which she tried calling once she'd figured out the confusing instructions on the motel phone. Dumb idea anyway, since her mom wouldn't have had time to drive home yet. It was all she could think to do, though. She couldn't call the police or a runaway hotline without putting herself in danger of revealing her wings.

A call from the front desk forced her to decide. "May I speak with Sarah McKenzie, please?"

"She's not . . . here right now," Linnet managed. Barely.

"When she gets back, please ask her to call the front desk. She was originally scheduled to check out today. There is a fee for late checkout. Or she can certainly extend the stay."

"I'll tell her," Linnet whispered, hanging up.

Now what?

Margaret McKenzie's address rested on the nightstand, next to the phone. As much as Linnet wanted to find out more about people with wings, she didn't want to go there alone.

But there was really nowhere else to go. And she didn't have to go in, after all. Maybe just ask some questions at the door. The old lady wouldn't dare drag her in, kicking and screaming.

Linnet dressed in the mosquito shirt and jeans, packing the rest of her clothes in her backpack. She wrote a note to her mother, simply "Gone to Grandmother's, Linnet." That didn't seem like enough, but she didn't want to mention Margaret McKenzie's name so anyone else could track her down. Besides, she had the awful feeling her mom wouldn't be back to read it. She put the crumpled notes from her mother in her backpack so no one could use them to follow her.

She couldn't get the idea of an old woman with a bottle of brandy and a knife out of her head. Before she left the room, she took the plastic letter opener from the drawer.

She half expected the man at the front desk to demand that she pay for the room instantly, but he ignored her as she went out.

A taxi had just unloaded a tall man's luggage. Before the driver could get back in, Linnet went up to him. "Can you take me to . . ." she handed him the paper.

He gave her a look, as if trying to figure out if she were running away. "My grandmother's house," she said. "My mother told me I could go visit while she was out—um—shopping."

Apparently that was good enough, because he opened the back door.

The taxi pulled up in front of a gray-blue house with black shutters. Linnet shivered and stared at the front door, gray with black trim and a half-circle window. "Is this the place?" asked the driver. He wore sunglasses when he drove, even though the sky was completely overcast. It gave Linnet the creeps to see those dark, blank eyes glancing at her in the rear-view mirror. "Is this the place?" he repeated.

She hesitated and then nodded.

"That will be four dollars."

Linnet felt herself turn pale. She had three dollars in her pocket. "I, uh, my mom forgot to give me—I have three dollars."

The driver pushed his sunglasses up on his head, gave her another look, and then sighed. "Yeah, I forgot to give you the kids' discount. Three dollars on the nose."

"Will you wait?" she asked. "I mean, in case she's—there's no one home?"

He gave her a nod and reached back to open the door for her. Then there was nothing to do but get out.

The path to the front door was edged with smooth stones, grays and whites and reddish browns, even some pinks. Closer now, she could see that the half-circle window had yellow curtains. *Be home, be gone, be home, be gone;* her thoughts wavered in rhythm with her steps. *Be home. Be gone.* The doorbell. She looked back to make sure the taxi was still there before she extended her finger. *Be home.* Touching the button, a quick jab. *Be gone.*

The yellow curtains fluttered. The top of a head and a pair of eyes looked out the window. Linnet's other hand grasped the letter opener in her pocket. A motor sound. The taxi pulled away as the door swung open.

When we walk to the edge of all the light we have and take
a step into darkness of the unknown, we must believe one of
two things will happen—there will be something solid for
us to stand upon, or we will be taught to fly.

—*Claire Morris,* Edges

CHAPTER

Three

Linnet stepped back. Her heels hung over the edge of the doorstep. Her breath stuck in her throat, coming so quick and shallow it never made it all the way down into her lungs. She hadn't planned what to say, how to tell who and what she was. But by the shock in the woman's eyes, that part wasn't necessary.

Her grandmother—who else could it be?—was a copy of her mother, only slightly aged. Lines on her forehead and a few streaks of gray in the short brown hair were the only differences.

They just stood for a moment, both paralyzed. Then, far from snatching Linnet in, Margaret McKenzie began to shut the door. "No," said Linnet. She dashed forward and pushed her way in.

As soon as the door closed behind her, she began to think it was a tremendous mistake. Suddenly, there was no air in the room, although it had been normal enough when she went in. The pale, wary face of her grandmother dissolved into black and white squares that swirled around until they were all black, black, black. Linnet flew into the black.

It must have only been seconds, for Linnet felt arms reaching into the darkness, catching her. The fabric of a print shirt came into focus before her eyes. Hands on her back, exploring her wings. "It can't be, it can't be," a soft chant in her ear.

Linnet pulled away. She remembered her mother and the knife and wanted to scream. If she had fainted for longer, would she have woken up with scar flowers on her back and a pain that would never go away? "Leave me alone," she said sharply. "I won't let you cut them off."

Her grandmother dropped to the floor. "I'm so sorry," she said, holding her face in her hands. Tears dripped out. "I didn't know what to do." She pulled her hands away and looked at Linnet. Her eyes looked older now. "Where's Sarah? She is your mother, isn't she? Is she here?"

The pain in the words and the eyes overwhelmed her, too much pain to bear. "She isn't coming," Linnet said. "She said you were a sadistic, cruel woman. She wishes you were dead."

New pain overlaid the old. The familiar face in the unfamiliar hairstyle turned away. Eyes closed, hard.

Linnet felt her throat closing. She fought to breathe normally, afraid to faint in the presence of this woman. And yet there seemed to be no threat to her.

"You are Sarah's daughter. What's your name?"

"Linnet."

Margaret laughed bitterly. "My granddaughter the bird. Maybe I'll be a better grandmother than I was a mother."

They didn't move, Linnet standing with her back to the door, the woman sitting on the entryway floor, clutching the faded rug in white fingers.

Linnet didn't know which question to ask first. Were there others? Why had she cut her daughter's wings off? She settled for "Can I have a drink of water?"

"A drink sounds good," said Margaret, standing up. Linnet followed her into a kitchen with ceramic tile counters and blue-striped wallpaper. Margaret ran water from the faucet into a glass with purplish blue irises painted on the side. Then she pulled a bottle from the back of a cupboard and poured herself a drink.

Linnet felt her mouth dry up in the middle of a sip of the none-too-cold tap water. She set her glass down and reached over, turning the bottle so she could read the label. Brandy.

She threw up in the sink.

Margaret's hands, small like her mother's, like her own, wiped her face with a wet paper towel.

"Why did you do it?" Linnet asked, standing again, only slightly wobbly.

Margaret's eyes went flat. "At that time, I didn't know what else to do," she said simply. "That's what my parents did to me. I couldn't see any alternatives."

Linnet backed against the counter. Her fingers found the letter opener in her coat pocket.

"At that time," Margaret repeated quickly. "I would never do it now, because—"

Her voice broke off and she seemed to be assessing Linnet, making a decision. "I would like to show you... a special place."

The car was an old Toyota. It jiggled along on the winding gravel road, making conversation difficult. Just as well, because Margaret had refused to tell her where they were going, and Linnet couldn't think of anything else to talk about.

Margaret had tried to get her to eat some soup back at the house, but Linnet hadn't been able to summon up an appetite at the time. Now she was hungry; her nerves and the jiggly road couldn't suppress that.

The road twisted around hills. Linnet felt as if she were motionless, with scenery sliding past her, teasing her with glimpses of animals and birds. Pine-dark mountains crept steadily nearer, like great stone beasts that breathed too slowly to perceive.

During the relatively straight parts of the road, when Margaret wasn't concentrating solely on her driving, she sneaked quick glances at Linnet, glances that seemed to say, *What exotic animal is in this car? Could this thing have come from what came from me? What the hell am I doing?*

Then she started talking, looking straight ahead. "I was eleven when I lost my wings." She laughed bitterly. "Lost— like one day I misplaced them. When my parents amputated them, before they had barely begun to exist. I never forgave them. I didn't want to do that to your mother. I thought if I bound her wings, they would stay small, we could hide them under her clothes, I wouldn't have to cut them off. But they kept growing, no matter how tightly I tied the cloth. I had to do it. I had no choice." She turned her head to Linnet for a second, read the answer there, turned back to the gravel road. "I didn't really expect you to understand."

Again the silence, only the sound of crushed rock crunching under the tires. The mountains had grown, were crouched before them. The road ran into the mountains' hearts and stomachs.

Linnet's own stomach growled.

"We'll be there soon," Margaret said simply.

Shortly, they turned onto a narrow, rutted road, the first sign that "there" was near. They were in the mountains now, or rather, in a valley between two great mountain beasts. Other, taller mountains loomed behind them, still snowcapped.

The valley floor was covered with slender trees with coin-shaped leaves that fluttered in the breeze. Not far from the road, a small, wild stream wandered between the trees and splashed over rocks.

Margaret caught Linnet looking at the trees. "Quaking aspen," she said. Her voice let Linnet know that they weren't going to talk about the loss of wings and whether it had been right or wrong. Linnet didn't know if she was relieved or angry. She did like knowing the name of the beautiful, shivering trees.

The valley and the road seemed to end just ahead of them. Was this the solution? To take her up into the mountains and leave her? Then the car topped the gentle slope and veered to the left, following the curve of the valley.

Ahead, a large house sprawled between the feet of the mountains. The center portion was made of old, weathered logs, with newer additions off to the sides—newer meaning weathered only to a silvery tan rather than outright gray. A long walkway sided with boards, glass bricks randomly placed in them, led from the left addition to a huge barn.

"We're here," said Margaret. "I hope..."

Whatever she hoped trailed off as a slender woman with untidy white hair strode up to the car. Hastily, Margaret lowered the window. "Margaret McKenzie—do you remember me?" she asked. "I have someone for you. My," her voice lowered, "granddaughter."

The woman's tight mouth relaxed into almost a smile, but her eyes remained sharp and knowing. She leaned into the open window and studied Linnet.

Linnet didn't like the way the woman's gaze seemed to pierce through the dark curtain of hair that hid her shoulders. She shifted in her seat, as far back as possible, which wasn't very far.

"Not a cutwing, then," said the woman. She turned her head and looked right into Margaret's face.

"No," whispered Margaret.

Linnet's stomach did a delirious flip to hear a stranger speak of wings. She must have made a noise, turned pale, given some indication of her unsettled state, because the woman said, "You'd better get her out of the car, into the fresh air."

Linnet didn't wait for anyone to help her. She fumbled the seat belt release with one hand and the door handle with the other.

Cool mountain air slapped her cheeks and made her feel better almost instantly. Margaret came around the car. "Linnet, this is Ellen Samuels."

Ellen gave Linnet a short nod. "I'm a cutwing," she said. "I take it you've heard of that?"

Linnet shook her head. "I know what it means, though." She shot a hostile glance at Margaret.

Margaret flinched. "I think I should go," she said.

"If you want," said Ellen. She looked hard at Linnet again. "Do you want to stay here?"

Thoughts raced each other around Linnet's mind. She didn't know where her mother was or if she'd find Linnet's note. She didn't have enough money to get home—or any way to get there safely even if she did. She did not want to go back to Margaret's house, to be in the place that had scarred her mother. But what did she know about this woman or this place? Not trusting herself to speak, she shrugged. Her wings needed to be freed. Could she do that here? "I don't know, I mean..." What if this was some sort of cult? "How do I know..." It was impossible to say what she was thinking.

Ellen's face ghosted a smile. "Let me put that another way: I would like you to stay for a few days. This is a good place for you. All right? Is this your bag?" She reached in through Margaret's open door and snagged Linnet's backpack without waiting for an answer.

Margaret's face held no trace of a smile, and Linnet could feel her own face draining of whatever expression it had held. "I'll take this into the house and be back out for you," said Ellen. She gave another of her apparently all-purpose nods. "Margaret." Looping the backpack over her shoulder, she turned and walked toward the house.

Silence quivered in the air like aspen leaves. Stretched. Fell. "If you need me..." said Margaret.

Linnet didn't answer. Couldn't answer.

Margaret closed the door Linnet had emerged from. She raised a small hand in a shaky wave as she walked around to her own side and got in. "If you need me..." she said again.

There was a wide graveled area in front of the barn. Margaret turned the car around and left.

I got wings, you got wings, All God's children got wings.

—Anonymous

*A bird's feathers normally weigh two
to three times more than its skeleton.*

—Pierre Gingras, The Secret Lives of Birds

CHAPTER

Four

Linnet felt as slender and slight as one of the shaking trees. After a few seconds, Ellen's hand closed gently around her arm. "Why don't you let me show you around."

Instead of the house, though, Ellen led her toward the barn. "This is what you need to see," she said, heading for a small door on the closest end of the building, near where the walkway joined the barn. She knocked on the door. "Just me," she hollered. "Somebody open up, please."

Linnet would have pulled back if not for Ellen's grip.

The door was opened by a stick-thin girl with dark skin and red-gold hair shaved close to her scalp. And wings. She looked as startled to see Linnet as Linnet was to see her.

"Linnet, this is Andrea," said Ellen. Without touching Linnet's back or shoulders, she propelled her through the door, into the spacious barn. Several other people were at the other end. At least two more of them had wings.

It's a dream, thought Linnet. Her legs turned to liquid, and she slid to the floor. Ellen caught her halfway down, and the dark girl helped.

Ellen's voice sounded far away. "Somebody run get a can of juice and some crackers or something." Linnet felt the girl's fingers steal a quick touch of her wings through the mosquito shirt. The sound of running feet. She was floating, sinking, drowning. Then the sweet, acid taste of orange juice. Ellen shoved a cracker into her hand. "Here, you can feed yourself."

Linnet obediently raised the cracker to her mouth. A small crowd had gathered around her. Ellen, Andrea, a to-die-for guy with golden brown hair and concerned eyes who looked about twenty-five, a solid woman who was maybe a little older than Linnet's mother, and, hanging back just a little, a boy, about six or seven probably, which meant not much smaller than Linnet. All of them, except Ellen and the kid, had wings.

Linnet's jaw muscles moved automatically, chewing the cracker, swallowing. Smooth, delicate wings with gray feathers emerged from the stocky woman's shoulders, too small for her sturdy body. White, twisted, deformed wings at odds with the young man's perfect looks. Most beautiful of all, Andrea's black wings. Chew, swallow. Sip, swallow.

"This is Linnet," said Ellen. "Her grandmother is a cutwing." She nodded to the stocky woman. "You've met her. Margaret McKenzie. Came up here looking for her runaway daughter."

The woman nodded. "I remember. About ten years ago? Maybe twelve?" She squatted down next to Linnet, obviously using her small wings for balance. "I'm Ellen's daughter, Jan. The boy over there is my son, Jake."

"Oh," said Linnet. "Hello."

"And I'm Charlie." The to-die-for guy seemed to be trying to fold his distorted wings, to make them small and unnoticeable.

"And you met Andrea," said Ellen.

The dark girl snorted. "Except you can call me Andy. Almost everyone does." Her voice held just the faintest tinge of hostility. Linnet couldn't tell if it was directed at her or at Ellen. The next words gave her a clue. "How come you got your wings so early?"

"I'm eleven," said Linnet quickly, a flush burning her cheeks. "I'm just small for my age."

Andy shot her a vicious glare, and Jan laughed. "Oh, poor Andy. Her goal in life is to be small for her age."

"Why would anybody want to be small for their age?" asked Linnet.

Jan's smile dissolved.

"You are so stupid," said Andy.

Linnet just looked around. Finally, Charlie cleared his throat. "Because," he said softly, "if you're small for your age, if you're light enough, you might be able to fly." He whirled around and almost ran into the walkway that led to the house.

"He forgot part of it," said Ellen. "If you still have your wings."

The boy, Jake, hadn't spoken yet. When his grandmother said this, with a bitter-tinted voice, he ran and gave her a hug. "It's okay, Grammy," he said. "I'll get wings someday, and I'll take you for a ride."

"Provided we're both small for our age," said Ellen. She ruffled his hair.

"I'm not going to be small for my age," he said. "I'll just have enormous wings instead."

Linnet was fighting with the feelings inside her. Elation at just being here. Fear. Disappointment tinged with hope. Since she was small for her age, she might be able to fly someday, but it didn't seem as if there were any guarantees. Her stomach growled.

"Come on," said Jan, standing up. "We'll show you your room and get you something to eat."

"I'm not sharing a room with her," said Andy.

Ellen gave Andy a level stare.

"Well, I'm not," said Andy.

"No one asked you to," said Ellen. "Quit being so rude."

"I think I'll go to my room," said Andy.

Ellen waited a few seconds after Andy had disappeared into the walkway, then headed that way herself, holding Jake's hand. "We'll get a room ready for you, Linnet."

Jan gave Linnet a hand up. "I'll bet you're dying to get those wings out."

Linnet nodded doubtfully. They did feel cramped and uncomfortable, but she would feel self-conscious walking around here with them exposed.

Jan gave her a sympathetic smile. "It won't be easy, of course, especially since everyone's going to be watching you carefully."

"Why?"

"Because we don't really know if any of us can fly. Andy's come the closest, but she's still heavier than her wings can manage, despite a careful diet and strenuous exercise regime. Poor Charlie never had a chance. And, well, I've never been small for my age." She looked hard at Linnet. "Maybe you'll be the first." Her smile turned a little lopsided.

The inside of the walkway was rough wooden planks that looked as if they were supposed to be that way. Black-and-white photographs—framed and unframed, tiny square prints, poster-size enlargements—were everywhere. One of the fluorescent fixtures had a bad tube; it flickered and buzzed, casting uneven, pale light as they walked through. Random rows of glass bricks interrupted the walls. They gave the illusion of outside without actually showing anything. It made sense, Linnet thought, if the walkway was for privacy, to keep the secret of wings from outsiders.

"Do other people ever come up here?" she asked.

"Nosy, suspicious people without wings?" Jan asked. "Sure. Sometimes. Mom advertises to attract people like you—cautiously worded, of course. There are a few weirdo journalists who think there might be a story, that maybe there's a secret enclave of winged people up in the mountains. Totally ridiculous, but some people will believe anything." She shook her head.

Linnet laughed.

Jan's voice lost its light tone. "And sometimes we've had fine people like my fifth-grade teacher, who came up to find out why my mother had pulled me out of school and moved to this remote area. Mom convinced her that I was being home schooled due to religious reasons. My wings were small enough then for me to hide them and talk to her and confirm that, but boy, was I tempted to tell her the real reason, and try living with wings in the real world." She sighed and her wings shook.

They were through the walkway now, in one of the newer parts of the house, which looked ordinary, except for all the photographs. Long, low shelves were crammed with books.

Then Jan led her across the big, log-walled living room that had probably once been the whole house. More photos—all framed—adorned the walls. "My mother's a famous photographer, in case you were wondering," she said. "That's one of the ways we pay our bills here. Plus it's fun, even for amateurs like me. Ellen'll have you behind a camera in no time, or stuck in the darkroom. She's a photography fanatic. I'm more into plants myself."

A monster spider plant, dripping with little green babies, hung in a glassless window that looked into a modern kitchen with an antique round table completely occupying one end. Linnet's stomach gurgled again.

"We'll make a pit stop here," said Jan. She opened up the fridge and rummaged around for a few seconds. "Where are a few decent leftovers when you need them?" The shelves on the refrigerator door were lined with film cannisters.

Linnet stared at Jan's wings and shivered. Could this possibly be real? Jan turned with a carton of milk in her hand. "Cold cereal?" she asked hopefully.

Linnet nodded. At this point, anything would be welcome.

"The cereal cupboard's behind you," Jan said.

There were fifteen or twenty boxes of cereal in the large oak cupboard, most of them open. Linnet let out a "Wow," and Jan laughed. "Cereal seems to be our main menu. It keeps pretty well and it doesn't take any time and even

Andy will eat it—provided we have skim milk." She plunked a green glass bowl and a spoon down on the table.

"Thanks," said Linnet. She chose a box of Cinnamon Life and sat down. She was starving, but her wings were killing her. She shifted in the chair as she poured milk over the cereal.

"I remember what it's like," Jan said softly. "Having to hide, needing so badly to move when you have to stay still."

Feeling so strange, Linnet wanted to say. Instead, she took a bite of cereal and forced it past the lump in her throat. After her stomach began to settle, her mind took over. "Why do we have wings?" she asked.

Jan absently wiped the front of the fridge with a dishtowel. "Why? Good question. It's apparently hereditary, but why?" She shook her head. "Since we haven't attracted a winged genetics expert—not likely, since wings seem to appear in fifth or sixth grade—we don't know much about the scientific side of things. Although maybe a cutwing... I'm afraid I don't have many answers for you."

"But..." Linnet started to say with her mouth full, then swallowed. She had more theories than that herself. "Is it like a mutation or something? Or"—this sounded stupid even to her, but she said it anyway—"or could we be aliens?"

"I don't know about mutations. That seems like a possibility. I sincerely doubt we're aliens, since we're so human in every other way." Jan finished wiping the fridge. She smiled and set the cloth down on the counter in a jumbled heap. "This isn't like me," she said. "My mother's the tidy one around here. And Andy. The rest of us—well, let's just say you're lucky to find the house in reasonable shape."

Looking around as she ate, Linnet began to notice bits and pieces out of order. Through the spider plant window, she could see a crumpled sock draped over the back of a rocking chair. A precarious pile of dirty dishes rose on the counter near the sink. She shifted position again, and a crunching sound made her look down. She had stepped on a piece of cereal, one of several that littered the floor under the table.

"It doesn't look so bad," she said, scooping up another spoonful from her bowl.

"So you're not a neatnik," said Jan. "Poor Ellen and Andy. They were probably hoping for reinforcements."

"I'm not a slob," said Linnet, with her mouth full. She swallowed. "And besides, I don't think Andy wants me here whether I'm neat or not."

Jan sighed. "Andy doesn't want anything but the ability to fly. She'll get used to you. Unless—" She broke off.

"Unless what?" asked Linnet.

"Nothing."

"That's not fair," Linnet muttered, glaring hotly into her bowl.

"You're right," said Jan. "I'm sorry. I was going to say,

unless you can fly and she can't. I doubt very much she could get used to that. Now can you see why I didn't want to finish my sentence?"

Linnet could see all right. And suddenly she didn't want to finish her cereal. "Where do I put this?" she asked. "Down the drain?"

Jan shook her head. "No. We don't use the garbage disposal any more than we have to. Not good for the septic system. We toss scraps out for the local wildlife. I'll show you."

She led Linnet out through the back of the kitchen, down a few steps, and around a clump of bushes. Corncobs, scraps of lettuce, and other kitchen leavings on top of a flattish boulder indicated that this was the place. "See that little hollow there? That's where we pour things like leftover cereal milk."

Linnet did so, feeling as if she were littering. "What eats the stuff?" she asked.

"Birds, chipmunks, deer, bears—"

"Bears?" Linnet looked around.

"Not very often," said Jan. "As long as you're making noise, you're okay. Isn't that right, bears?" she said loudly to the wilderness.

Linnet felt exhaustion fall on her. Everything—from sprouting wings to the trip with her silent mother to being abandoned in the motel to pushing into her grandmother's house to ending up here with bears—was too much.

"Come on," said Jan. "Let's get you to your room."

Back inside, they went up a staircase on the other side of the kitchen. "Mom and I have rooms in the other addition," said Jan. "And Jake. The rest of you are up here. That's Andy's room."

Linnet made a mental note never to knock on the closed door they had just passed. She had no burning desire to get her head bitten off.

"Charlie's room is at the far end of this hall, and if I'm right . . ." She opened a door. "I am. Mom stuck you in here."

Linnet's backpack sat on a chair at the foot of a twin bed with a faded green blanket over it. A short dresser under the window served as a nightstand. On top of it, near the bed, was a reading lamp and a small collection of books that rested between two large rocks. Plain, boring, ordinary, except for a narrow, rectangular photograph of a mountain range—half-illuminated, half in shadow—and the bright-winged butterflies hanging from a mobile over the bed. They danced in the slight disturbance made by the opening door. Linnet put up a hand, but she was too short to reach them.

"There's one of those with something winged hanging in every bedroom," Jan told her. "I think Charlie took his down. Some kind of birds maybe. I don't remember. In Andy's room there are—" She broke off. "You don't need to listen to me anymore right now. Take some time for yourself. Let your wings out. Just press the button on the doorknob," she said as she closed the door. "That locks it for you."

The butterflies twirled. Linnet pushed the button and pulled the shade down before she yanked off her sweatshirt and unfolded her wings.

The ache turned to a twinge of pain and then to glorious relief. Linnet flapped slowly as she tested out the confines of the small bedroom. She turned and leaned against the small dresser, supporting herself with her palms, and let loose with a wild frenzy of wings. The butterfly mobile went mad. Only when she was panting with exertion did she stop and dig through her backpack for the green halter-top. It was hard for her to put on now, trying to tie it behind her back with her wings in the way. What was she going to wear?

When she was dressed, the mobile still spun gently in the air. She looked in the round mirror that hung on the wall next to the door, reached up to touch a wingtip, straightened her hair a little. Her skin was pale as paper. She touched the doorknob for a second and then let go. She was just too tired. Too everything. She felt her eyes begin to fill up and closed them hard. She was not going to go out there.

She stood still until she felt as if she could open her eyes without causing a flood, then she flopped down on the bed and just lay there. A few tears leaked out. She closed her eyes again.

"Hope" is the thing with feathers—
That perches in the soul—

—Emily Dickinson

Five

A banging on the door woke her. Jan's voice. "Linnet? I've got some supper for you."

Linnet sat up and stretched. "Just a minute," she called. Where was her sweatshirt? She looked around and then stopped and took a deep breath. "Coming."

She stood in front of the door for a long moment before her hand turned the knob and slowly pulled. Her wings quivered. "Come in," she said.

Jan came in with a plate in one hand and a glass in the other. She looked Linnet over, but in such a frank way that it was strangely normal. "I can see why you were uncomfortable, with those wings all cramped up in a shirt. You've been asleep, haven't you?"

Linnet nodded. Her wings were suddenly a much smaller

part of her than her nose and mouth and stomach. She couldn't tear her attention away from the plate of food.

Jan laughed. "You're in luck," she said. "Charlie cooked tonight. Theoretically, we take turns, but at least half the time Charlie ends up rummaging through the kitchen and concocting something weird and wonderful. Mom does things like pot roast and potatoes, and Andy cooks mainly Bisquick pancakes. I do soup and sandwiches a lot myself. Homemade soup," she added, sounding defensive. "But Charlie—here I am talking too much again." She handed Linnet the plate and a napkin-wrapped bundle of silverware and set the glass on the dresser. "I didn't think you would want to come down to dinner yet."

"Thank you," said Linnet. Her stomach growled loudly.

Jan gave a smile and a wave and left, closing the door behind her.

The food on the plate did look odd, but it smelled great. Chopped-up meat in shiny sauce with a slightly orange tint to it. Green beans, left whole, that appeared to have been fried. Unpeeled baby potatoes, boiled, smashed with a fork, drizzled with butter, and sprinkled with a dark red seasoning. Even Bisquick pancakes would have been welcome. She shook the napkin over the bed and grabbed the fork that fell out. Before she had set the plate down on the dresser, she was eating.

It was all delicious, especially the meat, which tasted

sweet and strangely familiar. Linnet was still hungry after she finished. She didn't know the rules here, whether it was okay to get more, whether there was any left. She didn't really want to go downstairs with her wings sticking out.

She traced a figure eight in the sauce left on her plate and licked her fingertip. She couldn't stay up here forever. She didn't even know where the nearest bathroom was. She set the empty glass on her plate, gathered up her silverware and napkin, and opened the door with her free hand.

The hall was deserted, as was the stairway, but the noises from the kitchen drifted up. "Oh, Andy, just try some," she heard Charlie say. Andy muttered something that Linnet couldn't make out, and Jan laughed. Then Linnet was at the bottom of the stairs. Two more steps and she'd be in the doorway to the kitchen. "Hey, where's that girl?" Jake asked.

"She's having supper in her room," said Jan. "She's still tired from her trip."

Linnet stayed where she was, frozen. She couldn't go in now that they were talking about her. She lifted one heel; maybe she should just go quietly back upstairs.

Andy muttered again, just slightly louder, and Linnet could hear it this time: "What's so tiring about sitting in a car? It's not like she flew here."

"Andy," said Ellen, and then nothing more.

"I don't get tired in the car," said Jake. "I get sick and throw up."

Linnet moved forward suddenly, before they could start talking about her again. "Hello," she said. Her wings felt twice their normal size. "I was still hungry." Then she felt stupid. What if there wasn't any left?

Jan smiled. "Help yourself. There's an empty chair by Charlie. I'm afraid the potatoes are all gone."

"That's okay," said Linnet. They were all looking at her, but not nearly as avidly as she had imagined they would. She had to remind herself that they saw people with wings every day. Charlie scooted his chair a little to the side for her.

"Thanks," she said. She set her empty plate down on the table. "This was really good. Especially the meat."

"See," said Charlie, in Andy's general direction. Then to Linnet, "I cooked it with apricot syrup."

Linnet felt her eyebrows go up. "Apricot syrup?" she said.

"See," said Andy. She was on the other side of Charlie, and she poked him with a long, slender finger.

While this was going on, Ellen passed the plate of meat to Linnet. A small bowl with the last few green beans scattered in the bottom was already in front of her. "Finish it off," said Jan.

Linnet scooped up the beans and stabbed several chunks of meat with the fork from the plate.

"Some people," said Charlie, "know how to eat."

Andy stood up. "I know exactly how much I need to eat, and I'll eat that and no more," she said. She left the table, with her mouth set like stone. A few seconds later, they heard her door slam upstairs.

"Some people," said Jan, "don't know when to stop talking."

Charlie flushed. "Sorry," he said. "She just drives me crazy."

Jan sighed. "We've been through this before. She's not anorexic or bulimic—just highly disciplined and overly optimistic. She overdoes it sometimes, but she's not stupid and she's not sick. So leave her alone."

He nodded shortly. "Fine," he said.

Linnet didn't feel quite so hungry now, but she ate what she had dished out anyway. It did taste good.

Ellen took a sip of her coffee and looked at Linnet over the rim of the cup. "If you need to call anyone," she said, "there's a phone right by the fridge, or you can use the one in my bedroom. We do have some rules, though, for security. About revealing our location." She took another sip of coffee. "You can't tell anyone where we are or how to get here unless they have wings or had them at one time. And you have to clear it with me first."

Linnet lowered her eyes and pretended to be very interested in her plate, but as soon as the dishes were done, she went back through the big old room and began looking for Ellen's phone. The first room she poked her head into was obviously Jake's, unless someone else had an interest in Matchbox cars, and it made sense that the room next to his was Jan's. Anyway, there was no phone there. There were three more doors a little farther down the hall. One was a bathroom, so now she knew where there was at least one. Across from that was a medium-size room with dark green walls and an angel mobile. The phone was on the night-stand, resting on a copy of *Peter Pan*.

She held her breath as she went in and shut the door behind her, feeling as if she were trespassing even though Ellen had given her permission. The dark room pressed in on her. *She won't be home,* she thought, even as she dialed the number. *She won't be home, so why am I even calling?*

She heard the phone ring and ring and ring, not letting herself count. Loneliness and disappointment ate a hole in her. She had been expecting, somehow, to hear her mother answer. After more than a dozen rings, she hung up. The angels spun slowly in the air above her. Linnet glared at them and left.

When she slipped back into the big room, she heard voices in the kitchen—Jan and Jake and Charlie, playing a game of some sort, lively and laughing. She stopped and rested her head against the log wall, just below a picture of a frozen waterfall, half hoping she'd get a splinter. It was more than she could do to walk into that bright kitchen and be cheerful.

"If you want to mope," said a quiet voice, "this isn't the best place."

Linnet looked quickly about. Ellen sat in a rocking chair on the side of the room opposite the massive spider plant and the window into the kitchen. A tattered paperback rested in her lap, but the light was not really good enough for reading.

"I was just using the phone," Linnet said hastily, and immediately regretted it. Now there would be questions about whom she had called and what they had said.

"Ah," said Ellen. "Communicating with the outside world." And then nothing more.

Strangely, that made Linnet want to tell her. "I was just calling my mother, to tell—just calling my mother." She was not going to tell anyone that her mother had just dumped her in a motel with no options but a knife-wielding grandmother. That her mother had no idea where she was and how to reach her.

And that she had no way to reach her mother.

Jake's wild giggle erupted from the kitchen. "Now is that any way to treat your poor old mother?" protested Jan. "Sending me back to start?"

Linnet ran toward the warm light and through it, escaping up the stairs.

CHAPTER

Six

It was too early to go to bed, and besides, she'd slept most of the afternoon. She glanced at one of the books on her dresser, a picture book called *The Secrets of Animal Flight*, but she couldn't concentrate. The room wasn't big enough for a restless creature with wings. Linnet opened the curtain to let in the outside, give her more space. She pressed her face against the glass and caught a scream at the back of her throat.

A dark-winged figure, Andy, was sitting on the roof just to the right of her window. She was all lines and angles, except for the smooth curve of her wings. Her hair gleamed faintly in the dusk. She turned her head and looked at Linnet.

Caution and curiosity made Linnet release the bottom

catch on the window. She had to climb up on the dresser to reach the top catch before she could crank open the window. "What are you doing out there?" she asked.

"Sitting," said Andy.

Stupid question, thought Linnet. She should have just said hi or something.

She was trying to figure out what to say when Andy said, "Why don't you come outside?"

"On the roof? We could fall off."

"Fastest way of learning to fly," Andy said lightly.

"Are you kidding?"

"Of course I am, dope. You won't fall if you're careful."

Since she was already up on the dresser, it was easy to unhook the screen and take it out. She set it on the bed. Now there was nothing between her and the night. Suddenly, the room was more than big enough. Still, she stuck her right leg out onto the roof and slipped her wings through sideways, holding tightly to the window frame. The other leg now. She immediately lowered herself into a sitting position, her breath coming hard.

The air was cold against her bare skin, but she wasn't sure whether it was that or fear that inspired the goose bumps on her arms and neck and made her feathers fluff.

"Wouldn't you just love to leap off the roof and fly through the trees?" asked Andy, her voice low and dreamy.

Linnet said nothing. It was beautiful and frightening and wild. Stars were winking into view, blooming in the sky like diamond flowers.

Linnet shivered. "You can't do this in the winter," said Andy. "The roof is slippery with ice and the wind catches your wings and it's much too cold." She was shivering, too, harder than Linnet, who sat huddled in the slight protection of her long, tangled hair. There was a little wind now, playing with Linnet's wingtips, and her shivers turned to shudders as she imagined the wind ripping her from the roof.

"Do you really think we can fly?" she asked.

Andy stood up, angles straightening, becoming one graceful line. "I'm going in," she said, sliding through the rectangle of light with a smooth, practiced movement.

The window was miles, light-years away. Linnet sat frozen to the roof. The little wind tugged again.

Andy stuck her head out the window. "Aren't you coming in?"

Linnet nodded, but she didn't move.

Andy snorted. "Come in my window. I'll give you a hand."

Feeling stupid, Linnet scooted on her butt until she was directly below Andy's window. She took hold of the long-fingered hand that reached down to her and stood up shakily. Her feet seemed to be glued to the shingles, but she pulled one foot loose, with difficulty, and stuck it through the opening.

"Turn sideways more," Andy commanded.

Linnet complied, although that gave the wind a greater chance to catch at her wings. Andy gave a tug, and Linnet tumbled into the room. They both fell in a tangled sprawl of arms, legs, and wings.

"Ouch," said Andy, rubbing her shin where Linnet's knee had connected. "You might be small for your age, but—"

"I'm sorry," said Linnet, drawing her legs in and sitting up. "I didn't mean to—"

"I know," said Andy. "I did, though." She grinned ruefully, her teeth white. "I didn't bet on falling down myself when you did."

Linnet stared at her. She had meant to cause the fall.

"Close your mouth; flies will get in," said Andy. "That's what Ellen always says when someone looks surprised. Don't be surprised at anything I do," she continued. "I'm not someone who just goes around being nice for no reason." She brought her knees up and loosely circled them with one stick-slender arm. "So don't expect me to be nice and smiley when I don't feel like it."

"Fine," Linnet found herself saying defiantly. "Don't expect me to be either." She had to look away from Andy's face, which had gone from superior to surprised to appreciative in the time it had taken Linnet to speak.

The mobile above Andy's bed had tiny winged horses prancing in the wind from the still-open window. "Oh," said Linnet. "That's the best one yet."

"Yes," said Andy. "That's why I picked this room."

She was absently rubbing her shin through her jeans, and Linnet felt like apologizing again, even though she knew the whole thing was Andy's fault. Besides, Andy would think she was stupid if she did, so she stayed silent, pleased with this truce. If it wasn't exactly friendship, neither was it outright hostility.

Andy leaped to her feet. "It's freezing in here." She closed the window, reaching the top latch easily. Linnet watched her, studying the flare of her wings, the denim shirt with the back cut out. A frayed strip hung from the collar, covering the middle of her back. The bottom hem had been split up the center and was fastened back together with a safety pin. Linnet imagined how easily it would go on: Put it over the shoulders like a cape, letting the strip hang down between the wings. Button the front. Reach in back and pin the hem together.

The other girl turned around and caught Linnet staring at her. "I like your shirt," Linnet said, just as Andy's face was beginning to harden. "It looks warmer than a halter, but what do you do in winter?"

"Winter is tricky," said Andy. "If it's a little chilly inside, we drape big shawls over our wings. We don't go outside much, and when we do, we wear these blanket things. Jake calls them wing mittens. They're a pain to get on. You really can't do it yourself." She spun around, erratically. "And then the wind catches you and blows you around."

Linnet giggled, which surprised her as much as her earlier defiant statement. She simply wasn't—and had never been—a giggler. And to think antagonistic Andy had gotten her started.

The sound evidently reminded Andy that she was not thrilled to have an interloper around. "I'm tired," she said. "Get out of my room."

For a second, Linnet thought she would have to negotiate the roof again to get back to her open window. That was stupid, though. She gave Andy the smile that was all that remained of the giggle and opened the door. "Good night."

No answer. There was no one in the hallway, which was a little disappointing; no one to see her emerging from Andy's room as if they were truly friends.

She really had to go to the bathroom, and her teeth were gross. She went into her own room and dug her tooth-brush and toothpaste out of her backpack. Then she hesitated. It would be dumb to trek all the way down to the bathroom by Ellen's room if there was one up here. But she didn't want to go snooping around and maybe end up in Charlie's room by mistake. For all she knew, he could be in bed.

While she was thinking, Andy swooped down the hall. "Beat you," she called. She ran to open the farthest door on the left and closed it behind her.

Linnet smiled and sighed and sat down to wait.

Of course Peter had been trifling with them, for no one can fly unless the fairy dust has been blown on him.

—*J. M. Barrie,* Peter Pan

CHAPTER

Seven

The place was weird. Maybe no weirder than home, but then Linnet had never harbored any illusions about the normalcy of her childhood.

First there was the photography stuff. The darkroom, with its strange chemical smell, was near Ellen's room, adjoining the bathroom that Linnet had seen there. Brown plastic jugs of developing fluid neatly lined the shelf beside the door. On the shelf above them were boxes of unexposed photographic paper. Long strips of film were clipped on strings that looked like a mini-clothesline. A sink and a counter with a paper cutter and an enlarger ran along one side of the narrow room with its double entry. Just outside the darkroom, a glass-doored cupboard filled with cameras and flash attachments made the hall narrow.

Ellen had labeled one camera with Linnet's name and showed her how to load it. Linnet had taken only a few pictures so far, but it was fun, and she was anxious to finish off the roll. Ellen had promised to show her how to develop the film and make prints, too.

There were special prints in the darkroom—photographs of Jan, Charlie, and Andy in front of a wall with grid squares taped on it. A few were of Charlie and Andy, but most were of Jan, charting the growth of her wings from when she was no older than Linnet. It gave Linnet an odd feeling to look at those pictures, especially the first few, when Jan's wings were tiny. It seemed like spying, like violating a trust, and yet it didn't seem to bother Jan in the least. You got used to anything, Linnet supposed, even wings.

She was looking at the prints when Ellen came into the darkroom. "I didn't know anyone was here," she said, blinking her eyes in the amber light.

"I was just..." Linnet stopped. Maybe she wasn't supposed to be in here alone.

Ellen didn't seem to mind. She looked at the prints of the others. "We need to get you photographed," she said. "I like to keep a record—take a photo every few months." She touched the first one of Jan and smiled; rather wistfully, Linnet thought. "We thought she'd be able to fly," she said.

There was nothing Linnet could say.

Ellen looked at her. "How are you doing?" she asked. "Do you want to stay here? I could take you back to your grandmother's."

"No," said Linnet. She wanted to plunge into the story of what had happened in Livingston, but she couldn't. Loyalty to her mother? "I'll just stay for a while, if that's okay." If it wasn't, she didn't know what she'd do.

Ellen gave her a quick smile. "It's okay. But if you're done here, Jan's looking for someone to play checkers with Jake."

They left the darkroom. Ellen took a camera and flash from the cupboard and selected a few screw-on filters, which she put in one of her vest pockets. "It will all work out," she said.

Linnet hoped so.

When Ellen had Linnet stand next to the gridded wall the next day, Linnet felt as if she were having a mug shot taken. Ellen took shots from the front, back, and both sides. "There," she said briskly. "I just have a few more frames left on this roll. I'll let you know when it's done, and you can help me develop it. Okay?"

Linnet nodded and went off to find something to do until then. She didn't really want to be alone, so she went to the barn. As usual, Andy was there.

Andy was an exercise fanatic. She ran around and around the barn, lifted weights, and flapped her wings in a frenzy, taking timed breaks to eat precise amounts of bread or cereal or yogurt or fruit. Linnet had tried running with her, but Andy's legs were so much longer than hers, and Andy wouldn't modify her pace for anyone. Linnet watched for a while, then wandered back through the walkway into the house, still thinking about the others. Maybe Charlie needed some help in the kitchen.

Charlie worked out, too, but not when Andy did. He was fun, because he liked to visit while he lifted weights or jogged, and he would slow down to Linnet's speed. When she first arrived, all she could think about was how gorgeous he was, but it didn't take long to figure out he was more than twice her age. She spent a fair amount of time with him, but his wings made her queasy sometimes, called up the memory of her mother, whose wings had been bound before they were removed.

She had tried calling home eight more times. Still no answer. Then, on the ninth try, she got the "Sorry, this number has been disconnected" message. What if something had happened to her mother? She called the motel, and the guy there said they had no such guest registered. When she tried the copy shop and asked for Sarah McKenzie, the chirpy woman on the other end said, "I don't know anyone by that name. Perhaps she works at a different location?" She even called Margaret McKenzie once, to find out in a roundabout fashion whether Sarah had been in contact with her. No luck. Margaret sounded uneasy, and Linnet didn't know what to say either.

Jan and Jake and Ellen — they were a normal family — except that one of them had wings and one of them used to have wings and one of them might have wings someday. Sometimes seeing them together made Linnet alternately ache or seethe with anger. She deserved a better grandmother than Margaret, and a mother who wouldn't desert her.

What she had told Andy — *Don't expect me to be nice for no reason* — was a lie, though, for she kept on being nice, smiling when she didn't feel like it, doing dishes, throwing scraps out for the animals.

That was the job Charlie gave her now — taking a bucket of potato peels, coffee grounds, eggshells, and miscellaneous bits of food out to the boulder. It didn't feel like littering anymore, and it was especially fun when there were deer hanging around. If she moved slowly and carefully, they didn't move off very far, just waited for her to dump the stuff and leave.

This time, when Linnet saw the deer, she decided to stay and watch. She emptied the bucket on the boulder and slowly walked to a basketball-size rock about twenty feet away. There were four deer: a doe, two fawns, and a little spike buck who was probably the fawns' big brother. They all watched her sit down on the rock, their big ears upright and alert. Linnet just sat there, not moving, and after a minute the doe flipped her ears and started walking toward the boulder, freezing every few steps to make sure Linnet didn't pose any danger.

As soon as the doe began nosing the food, the fawns followed her. The spike buck seemed more interested in Linnet. He took several cautious steps toward her. She held her breath. He came closer.

The scrap bucket was right in front of Linnet's feet, with a few curls of potato peel still stuck to the sides. She sat frozen. The deer came nearer. Stopped. Took another step. Linnet didn't move, even when he had almost reached her. She felt as if she didn't need to breathe. The little buck put his nose down toward the bucket, lifted his head sharply, and looked at her. Still she didn't move. He put his head in the bucket and used his tongue to snag a potato peel, his lower jaw moving from side to side as he chewed.

When he was done with that, he got another peel, in the process moving the bucket until it was stopped by Linnet's feet. His head was right in front of Linnet's when he lifted it, and he paused to look at her before flicking his ears and joining the other deer at the boulder.

Linnet took a breath and grabbed the bucket handle. Very smoothly, she backed away and started toward the house. Ellen was standing by the back door with a camera. She nodded to Linnet and opened the door for her. "I'm glad I put new film in the camera before I came to find you," she said. "I think I got some excellent shots."

"He came right up to me," said Linnet. "He wasn't scared."

"Well, you're not very scary, are you?" said Ellen. "Do you want to help me develop that other roll?"

Ellen closed the darkroom door behind them and flipped on the warning light outside. "Never burst in here when that's on," she said. "And never open the inside door unless the outer one is closed." She got out something that looked like a stainless steel roller. "I have to shut off all the lights for a minute, while I get the film in." It felt odd to be in total darkness. "Okay, I've got the top on. Turn on the light switch on the far right and grab that big brown jug that says developer on the front."

Ellen instructed her on the amount to pour in. "Now just turn it over at least every thirty seconds to keep the fresh chemicals circulating around the film. We'll keep this up for about five minutes." The next step was the stop bath, which worked immediately, and then the fixer, which took another five minutes or so. Ellen opened the developing container and put the film in the film washer. Water bubbled up from underneath for five or ten minutes. "Now," she said, "let's see what we've got." She held a strip of film up, touching only the edges. "Look at this," she said, pointing. "Here's the first one of you, with your back to the camera."

It looked strange, with her dark hair showing up light and her skin dark.

"We'll leave these to dry," said Ellen, clipping the film to a string and running a little squeegee over both sides, "and print them later. That's the really fun part."

And it was. First they did a contact sheet, cutting the film into strips and placing it into a contact easel with an eight-by-ten sheet of photographic paper. The glass top of the contact easel pressed the film and paper together. They exposed it under the enlarger for five seconds. "This way we can pick which images we want to enlarge and print," Ellen said. Then she had Linnet swish the photographic paper back and forth in the chemicals.

"Wow," said Linnet, grinning, as the images formed before their eyes. "This is so cool."

"Now switch it to the stop bath," Ellen told her.

Linnet picked the paper out with plastic tongs. "Is this right?"

"You're a natural," Ellen said. "The smell doesn't even seem to bother you."

Linnet sniffed. "It does smell," she said, "but I kind of forgot about it."

The fixer was next, then rinsing the paper off with plain water. Then they got down to choosing the frames, setting up the enlarger for the desired size and exposure time, putting in an unexposed sheet of photographic paper, and exposing it. The first shot they enlarged was a profile of Linnet against the gridded wall.

They printed all the photographs they wanted from the roll and hung them up to dry, again using the squeegee. A bunch of negatives hadn't turned out at all, but Ellen didn't seem upset. "Sometimes I shoot a whole roll and get one good picture," she said. "You just have to live with it. I hope the ones with you and the deer turn out well, though. The lighting was excellent, and the setup might be hard to re-create."

She looked at Linnet, amber-tinted and serious. "I hope you're happy here. If there is ever anything you want to talk about..."

Linnet swallowed. She definitely had questions, and if anyone had the answers, it would be Ellen. "Do you think there are many other people like us?"

Ellen looked down. "I'm sure there must be. But does it matter that much? It's not as if every person with wings is going to be a good person. Do you really want to know everyone who has wings? Here, use the funnel to pour the stop back in the jug. We can reuse it."

She let it go at that, and Linnet just nodded and helped hang the photos and clean up.

The weirdest thing about being here was not the winged people or the fact that the garbage disposal had legs. It was the "permanent temporary" feeling. There wasn't any real school, although there were enough books to rival a school library. Linnet had looked through quite a few of them. Someone—Jan maybe?—had printed a list of page numbers and titles that had something to do with wings or flying. But there was nothing she *had* to do. It was summer, though, and maybe things would be different in the fall, with actual lessons and assignments and study time.

Linnet didn't want to ask. She didn't want to think of being here, but she didn't want to think of going back to a place where she would have to hide. Or where she couldn't hide unless she had her wings amputated.

This situation just didn't seem real: an oddly mismatched group of people brought together, with the exception of the three who were related, by a deformity. No, not a deformity. The beauty of their wings would not allow her to think of them that way. A transformation. Half of them were waiting around to see whether they could fly. Half never would, but somehow they were always waiting, too. Waiting to grow wings back or grow wings straight or lose enough weight for wings to lift an intentionally slender body.

And everyone, it seemed, was waiting to see whether Linnet could fly.

Especially Linnet.

The edge of the loft seemed very high above the thick mat that covered a strip in the center of the barn floor. The cable that went from the post to the far wall of the barn looked spindly. "You're sure this will hold me?" asked Linnet. Her hands were slippery on the handles of the plastic device that was attached to the cable.

Andy gave the cable a twang that undulated away from them. "If it doesn't hold you, it won't hold anyone—and I'm still here, aren't I?"

"I guess."

"Believe me, I'm here. And so are you, which is the problem. You're supposed to be down there."

Charlie was below them, a little off to the side, giving a thumbs-up signal. Ellen stood more in the middle of the barn, with a camera, of course. Jan and Jake waited near the point where the cable attached to the wall. "I don't think—" Linnet began.

"Good," said Andy. "Thinking is a bad idea. It's better to just jump off. Get your wings flapping before you jump."

"I—"

"Start flapping."

Linnet started. *Oh, please,* she said to herself, not sure whether she was asking for the guts to stay on the loft in the face of Andy's contempt or the guts to launch herself into space. Then Andy swept one long leg out and knocked her off the edge.

If the Milky Way were not within me
how should I have seen it or known it?

—*Kahlil Gibran,* Sand and Foam

CHAPTER

Eight

Linnet's wings faltered, just for a second, then restarted, beating in a frenzy. She almost lost her grip as she swooped down past Charlie. Were the wings giving her some lift? It was hard to tell, hard to separate her efforts from the dizzying rush of the glider.

She was slowing now, nearing Ellen, who was snapping photos like mad. Linnet kept flapping fiercely. Without the speed to confuse her, it did seem as if her wings were helping. Jake was jumping up and down, clapping and yelling.

Her arms were almost falling off when she made her wings propel her up the little slope at the end. She let go, and Jan half caught her. They fell over onto the strip of mat that ran down the middle of the barn floor.

"She did it! She did it!" Jake screamed. "Yahoo!"

"Cool it, buddy," said Jan, sitting up.

The cable jerked over them, and Andy swept toward them, her wings arched during the first dive and then beating slowly and powerfully. Before Linnet could scramble out of the way, Andy dropped to the mat, inches from her. "You looked like a mad chicken," she said.

"Well, I did it," said Linnet hotly.

"With a little help," said Andy. She lazily swung one long leg in a kicking motion.

Linnet just glared at her.

"Enough, Andy," said Jan. "How did it feel, Linnet? Any lift?"

"I think so," said Linnet. "It felt like it at the end."

"Lift? Or just forward momentum?" asked Ellen, who had reached them by then.

"Looked like forward momentum to me," said Andy.

Linnet wanted to contest that statement, but she truly didn't know the answer. She just shrugged.

Andy let her great wings flare. "If you want to try again," she said, "let me know. And don't flap so fast." She walked back toward the loft.

Linnet wanted to explode or cry—or really fly, just to show Andy. Jan gave her a quick pat and a rueful grin. "She's hard to take sometimes, like all good medicine."

"Or like poison," said Linnet.

After that, Linnet didn't have to be pushed off the loft.

She went again and again, learning the best angle to hold her wings for the initial dive, the optimum flapping speed. She concentrated on the yellow plastic grip in her hands, willing herself to feel a lessening of pressure, some evidence that she was actually flying, lifting herself into the air.

Nothing more than forward momentum.

If that was all of life—fun but futile glides from the loft, wondering whether she'd ever see her mother again—the summer would have worn heavy. But there were also evening games with Jan and Jake and Charlie. Charlie especially loved games: Aggravation and Monopoly and Pictionary. He even taught her to play chess, but he wouldn't play Trivial Pursuit unless everyone else ganged up against him. "I'm a storehouse of useless knowledge," he always said. "It just wouldn't be fair."

She played alone with Jake, too, kid stuff such as building forts, racing monster trucks, playing hide-and-seek. Jan acted as if this were a big favor, like baby-sitting, but Linnet had more fun than she would have admitted to anyone.

And then there were the unpredictable, dizzying times with Andy. Frequently, Andy ignored her or worse. Teased her about her hair, which was always escaping from the braid Linnet wore now that she didn't have to hide her wings: "I know why you can't fly; your hair weighs a ton." Yelled when Linnet merely knocked on her door: "Leave me alone. Don't you know when a door is shut it means that somebody wants to be left alone?"

Most of the time, Linnet hated her, or wanted to anyway. She didn't have to be so mean. Or, if she was going for the Miss Nasty title, why did she suddenly show up on the roof outside Linnet's room on a full moon night, scritching on the glass and smiling, leading Linnet out into a magical wild world of glitter-eyed deer and pine-scented air?

There was a meadow not far from the house, with two oblong rocks sprawled in the center of it. They almost always went there. If it wasn't too late, the rocks still held a little of the heat from a day of sunning.

Andy's rock—of course, she got the best one, since she had found them—was a massive oval slab, pale gray, with little flecks of some sparkly stuff in it that glinted even in moonlight. Smooth. Half again as long as Andy when she lay stretched out on it, a dark figure against the pale surface. Linnet's rock was smaller, though still long enough for her to lie full-length. Rougher, too, the pale gray material of Andy's rock mixed with another, darker material.

Another weird thing about Andy was how you couldn't tell from her mood one minute how she'd act the next. Tonight was a perfect example, Linnet thought, crouching at the edge of the roof where a trellis made an ideal ladder. Andy had been a total pain all day. Then, just when Linnet was about to fall asleep, she knocked on the window, illuminating her grinning face with a flashlight. There was no moon—or just a tiny sliver—so Linnet hadn't expected her. "That's why we have this," Andy said, shining the flashlight into Linnet's eyes. "I thought we'd try stargazing. Coming?"

And, of course, the only answer to that was to slip out the window.

The bobbing flashlight beam stabilized, signifying that Andy had reached the bottom. A helpful splash of light traveled up the side of the house and stopped at Linnet's feet. She turned and let herself down, feet made comfortable by practice. Not that she was ever totally comfortable in Andy's presence; practice didn't seem to help on that account.

As if to validate her uncertainty, the light snapped off. "Dark, huh?" Andy whispered.

Linnet stifled a cry. At least Andy couldn't see her shiver. "Yeah," she replied, equally low. "Look at the stars."

"Not here, stupid." Andy's voice was a little farther away now. "At the rocks. Coming?"

Linnet made her voice steady. "Not unless you turn on the light."

Andy laughed, and the splash of light was back, moving along the ground between them, deforming as it traveled over rocks and clumps of weed, momentarily coloring wildflowers. "Don't get left behind," she said.

"I won't," said Linnet, hoping rather than believing her own words. She dashed forward, following the light.

It didn't take them much longer than usual to reach the rocks, but Linnet was panting uncharacteristically when she got there. She'd been holding her breath for a good portion of the time, she decided, flopping down on her rock, taking comfort from the vestiges of warmth there.

Andy killed the light. Stars hung over them like chips of diamond. "Wow," said Linnet. She spread her wings wide and carefully lowered herself onto her back. She couldn't sleep that way, of course, but it was okay for short periods. "Do you know the constellations?"

"What difference does it make?" said Andy. She sounded half-angry. "Does it make them any prettier to know what some dead guys thought they ought to be called?"

"No," admitted Linnet. It was true, she thought, that knowing the names wouldn't make the sky any more beautiful. Her own knowledge didn't extend past the Big Dipper; that group of stars wasn't any lovelier than the rest. Silence seemed safer now, even if she did agree.

After a few star-soaked minutes, Andy spoke up again. "So what's with your folks?"

Linnet tensed up. "What do you mean?"

"It's no news that you're not exactly getting care packages," said Andy. "And you used to keep sneaking off to Ellen's room and looking like some lost puppy when you came back. But you don't do that anymore. So what's with them? They dump you?"

The rock scraped against Linnet's left arm and wing as she rolled over onto her stomach. Her eyes burned with sudden, angry tears. Damn Andy for noticing. They probably all had, probably talked about her behind her back. Damn Mother for... She shied away from the end of that sentence. "Quit spying on me," she said, her voice thick with rage. "Tell the rest of them, too."

Andy gave a nervous laugh. "Hey, I'm the only sneak in the bunch," she said. "The others are too nice. Must have been the way they were brought up."

There was some unexpected bitterness in Andy's voice. When Linnet could trust her own voice, she said, "What about your parents?"

"What about them?" Definitely bitter. "My so-called mom tried to sell me to the circus, and I never met my dad, but he's probably a creep, too."

"I never met my dad either," said Linnet. There was so much to respond to that she didn't know where to start. "Your mom tried to sell you to the circus? Did she have wings?"

"Her? She would have sold herself to the circus if she had. Must have been my dear old daddy. He must have been a cutwing. Unless I'm an original. After all, wings have to start somewhere."

Linnet tried to see Andy's face in her mind, because her voice had lost all expression by that point. Was it safe to keep asking questions? She decided to keep it up until Andy told her to quit. "So how come you're here, then, instead of the circus?"

"Because the ad that my mom answered wasn't really from the circus—it was Saint Ellen, trying to save the world. Or at least the part of the world that has wings."

"Your mom sold you to Ellen?" That thought made Linnet uncomfortable.

"Kind of," said Andy. "She was going to, but Ellen got me alone and told me about the place, and I ran away with her instead. I bet my mom went into a rage." Some cheerful spite crept into her disembodied voice.

"Isn't your mom looking for you?" Linnet could just imagine the FBI descending on the place. Her skin prickled.

"What could she say? That the daughter she was trying to sell to the circus ran away? Can't you just see my picture on a milk carton: 'Look for a tall, dark, skinny fourteen-year-old with wings, last seen running away from the circus.'"

Linnet let out a tiny giggle before she could stop it, but Andy didn't seem to mind. They lay there in the darkness for a while.

Linnet didn't decide to tell Andy; she just started talking. "My mom left me in Livingston. Just left me. It was my grandmother who brought me up here." She hesitated for a second, and the words poured out. "She cut my mom's wings off with a knife."

"And I thought my mom was a bitch," said Andy. "I'm glad she wasn't around to take lessons from your grandmother."

"How did you hide your wings?" asked Linnet, after another silence had stretched out thin between them.

"My mom just kept me home after they sprouted. Told everybody that I was real sick—contagious. I had to quit school and everything."

"You don't sound like you quit school," said Linnet.

"That's because I'm smart," said Andy. "Ellen gets all these books for me, but I don't read much in the summer, except science fiction. Ellen says everybody should get a summer vacation."

Linnet felt the darkness come down on her hard. Living here was starting to feel real, and that was frightening. She still didn't know where her mother was or if she'd ever see her again. Was she going to be here forever?

"I said," Andy's voice broke in, impatient, as if she'd been talking to Linnet for a long time, "how did you hide *your* wings?"

"Uh, I didn't have them very long and I just let my hair cover them up and then I came here." That summary didn't seem to have anything to do with the shock of developing wings and her mother's revelation and the awkward trip to Margaret's and coming here.

"So did your mom dump you?" Andy asked again. "I mean, like she's not coming back?"

"Shut up," Linnet screamed, sitting up, fists clenched. "You don't know anything about it."

"That's because you won't tell—"

"Shut up, shut up, shut up." Linnet's voice quivered with rage.

Andy was silent. The night was silent. The stars blurred and swam together in the tears that coated Linnet's eyes. She knew that it wasn't just Andy she was mad at, that she was incredibly angry at her mother for taking off. Apologies stuck in her throat, though.

She flopped down on her stomach and let the tears drip. The rock was rough against her face, and she was glad. It seemed like a long time before there was nothing left of her outburst but the tight feeling of salt dried onto her cheeks. "Andy?" she said, not sure what she was going to follow that with.

But there was no answer. No flicker of a flashlight. Andy was gone.

Scientists believe that birds take advantage of natural clues to navigate. Those that fly at night use the position of the stars, just as oldtime sailors did. Birds also detect the invisible magnetic field that surrounds the earth.

—*National Audubon Society First Field Guides: Birds*

CHAPTER
Nine

The wiped-out feeling disappeared, replaced by a fresh wave of anger. And fear. It was dark, the jeweled starlight giving only the faintest clues about object and direction. If she tried going back now, she could fall and break a leg. Or get lost, wandering away from the house rather than toward it.

Maybe she should stay where she was and go back at dawn. That would mean staying out all night, alone except for all the wild animals. Suddenly, the night didn't seem so silent. Whispers and rustles—the wind? Or something alive? Even deer didn't seem so benign to her now.

She started to shiver. It could get cold out at night, too, even in the summer. What if she got hypothermia? Would Andy even tell anyone where she was?

The shapes of trees were like darker cutouts in the blackness, visible mainly because they blocked the stars. They loomed about her, outlines shifting in the breeze. "Damn," she whispered. Swearing didn't help. Didn't hurt either. She said it louder. "Damn."

Something like a groan sounded from near Andy's rock. Linnet froze and pressed herself harder against the rough surface of her rock. She tensed her muscles and got ready to run, all the while reminding herself that she still couldn't see to run. Whatever was over there could probably smell her fear and hear the sound of her racing heart and would have no trouble seeing in the dark. She wished she were as dark as Andy, so she wouldn't provide such a clear target.

The thought caught in her mind. How could Andy have gone so quietly? Linnet hadn't had her eyes closed the whole time, and she would have seen the flashlight if it had been turned on. And if it hadn't . . . Andy was some kind of wonderful, but she couldn't see in the dark any better than Linnet could.

She was still here.

Probably on the ground on the other side of her rock. When Linnet swore out loud, Andy had tried to stifle a laugh, and it had sounded like a groan.

Linnet sat up, very slowly. She eased her legs over the side of the rock until her feet touched the ground.

Andy's rock was about two steps from hers at the closest

point. Linnet took in three quiet breaths and leaped. The grass rustled when her feet hit, but she was on Andy's rock and over the other side before she could even worry about the other girl hearing. She scraped her knee on the rock going over, but there was barely time to notice that either, before she landed and Andy screamed.

And then they were both laughing hysterically, sprawled side by side on the ground. "You idiot," Andy gasped. "You practically killed me."

"Yeah, right," said Linnet, injecting as much sarcasm as possible. "I'm not the one who pretended to leave."

Andy giggled. "It was a good joke, wasn't it?"

"It was not." But Linnet wasn't mad anymore. She had passed some sort of test. How could she stay mad at Andy, when Andy was the reason for the test? It would be like being mad at a racetrack for making you tired after you'd just won a race.

"Let's go back," said Andy. "I'm getting cold."

So was Linnet, but she didn't want to leave now, when she'd just tamed the wild night with her leap. And earned Andy's admiration. "In a minute," she said. She adjusted her position a bit to relieve a cramp in one wing. "I want to look at the stars a little while longer."

"Fine," said Andy. "Freeze us to death stargazing. See if I care." She didn't get up and walk away, though.

Linnet just lay there, irrationally pleased by the feel of grass and pebbles poking her back and wings. Andy's rock bulked beside them, but it was a familiar bulk.

"Done communing with nature yet, O pale one?" Andy inquired. "Would it offend your royal retinas if I turned on the flashlight?"

Linnet sensed that Andy was holding said flashlight right in front of her face. She grinned. "Go ahead," she said, rubbing her arms and shutting her eyes. "The royal retinas are prepared."

There was a click, and Linnet flinched, but there was no corresponding bloom of pink indicating light filtered through eyelids.

"Oh, shit," said Andy softly. "I think you broke the flashlight."

Linnet's eyes squeezed shut tighter and then opened. "Let me see," she said, grabbing for it.

"You can't see," said Andy. "That's the whole point. If you'd like to feel—ouch, you scratched me."

"Sorry," Linnet muttered as her hands moved over the flashlight she had just snatched. She pushed the button several times. Nothing.

"Oh, great," she said. "Now what are we going to do?"

"Walk back and fall off a cliff on the way," said Andy. "Bury ourselves in pine needles to keep warm and get eaten by rabid termites or something. Start screaming and hope that Ellen is out taking a midnight walk—with a working flashlight."

Nothing fazed Andy. Linnet felt half-okay about being

out in the dark half a mile from the house. Half-okay.

They lay there silently for a minute, then Linnet rolled over. The ground was much less comfortable now that her bed wasn't an option. "What time does it get light?" she asked.

"Five, six, something like that," said Andy. "I never get up then, so I'm not sure."

"And it's about midnight now?"

"Or eleven."

The conversation petered out again. *Five hours at least,* Linnet thought. Five hours—or six, or seven—to get cold and be uncomfortable and hear noises. She groaned.

Andy imitated her, adding a whuffing noise at the end of her groan. Linnet let out a soft, mournful howl.

Before Andy could contribute another noise, a strange, male voice said, "What was that?"

Linnet and Andy shrank together, huddling in closer to the massive rock.

"A coyote?" Another voice—a woman's. Scratchy, as if she smoked. "Maybe. I don't know. It sounded kind of strange, though. I think there are coyotes and bears and things around here. Why couldn't you have picked a more civilized area—like maybe Boston?"

By now, Linnet could see random splashes of light playing over the pines. She clutched Andy's arm tighter. Andy was shaking, maybe with suppressed laughter. Linnet put a stern finger up to Andy's mouth.

"Because," the first voice answered, "this is where we tracked down the addresses for the ads." Linnet felt Andy go completely still.

"Do you really think we're going to find freaks with wings up here?"

"I don't know. It makes a change from Elvis sightings and UFOs, though."

The voices passed by on the other side of Linnet's rock. She scarcely breathed, lying frozen beside Andy.

"We'll get the camera set up in the trees behind the house." There was a loud yawn. "Then we can take turns sleeping for a few hours."

"Unless the bears get us."

"Deer and coyotes and bears, oh my!"

"Yeah, yeah."

The lights and voices disappeared into the pines, but it was a long time before either of the girls moved. "What are we going to do?" hissed Andy.

"We just have to get back before it gets light," said Linnet. "And we can't run into those reporters."

Andy clunked her on the wrist with the broken flashlight. "How are we going to do that? We don't exactly have a yellow brick road to follow. 'Deer and coyotes and bears, oh my!'" she imitated.

Linnet's mind clicked. "The stream. We'll go until we find the stream, and we can follow it to the driveway. We'll just have to go slow."

Andy sounded a little less skeptical, but still not totally convinced. "How are we going to make sure we run into the stream?"

"We go from my rock, in a straight line." That sounded stupid to Linnet even as she said it. "We don't have to go exactly straight anyway, because it doesn't matter where we hit the stream."

"You're right," said Andy. "Then we just head downstream, and when we reach the driveway, we're in front of the house. The reporters will never see us."

"Ellen," said Linnet, "is going to kill us."

Andy groaned. "You're right. And then she's going to give us a medal, because otherwise those jerks would have taken pictures of Jan emptying the garbage or something." She rattled the flashlight. "It's a good thing you broke this, because otherwise they could have just followed us and got pictures of us climbing up to our windows. I can just see the headlines: WINGED HUMANS HUNT AT NIGHT."

"You think they're going to claim us as humans?"

"WINGED CREATURES, maybe."

Linnet felt curiously cheerful. "How about SECRET WINGED SOCIETY PLOTS TO OVERTAKE THE EARTH. LOCK ALL WINDOWS?"

"And, of course, the article would conveniently forget to mention that we can't fly." A bitter note crept into Andy's voice.

Linnet stood up. "Come on. We've got to get back, and it's going to take us a while in the dark."

That was an understatement. Linnet began to wish she were a bat, even a flightless bat. Sonar would have been useful, she thought, as she scraped her leg on another small rock. Andy kept up a steady stream of muttered curses, intermixed with occasional yelps as she was attacked by various vegetables and minerals—fortunately, no animals, unless you counted mosquitoes. Linnet did her own share of yelping as well, although they both tried to be quiet.

They heard the stream, and smelled it, before they reached it. Fresh and merry, even in the middle of the night. There were faint glints among the trees, but they were not entirely revealing, Linnet discovered, as she stepped into the icy water with a splash. That inspired a bigger yelp than usual. Andy started to laugh, and then she blundered into the creek, too.

It was a good thing the reporters were more at home in Boston than they were in the Montana wilderness.

By the time they reached the driveway, Linnet's ankles and feet were frozen. One cheek had a scratch from a branch. She was exhausted from jumping at shadows and noises, thinking that any minute now, a reporter would leap out and take a flash photo, saying, "Smile, you're in the *National Enquirer.*"

Andy was in similar shape, limping from a twisted ankle.

That slowed them down on the final approach to the house, but Linnet didn't want to leave Andy hobbling through the darkness alone. Finally, they reached the house.

It was locked, of course. Linnet hesitated, her finger poised over the doorbell. Ellen in the middle of the night. She was not exactly stern, and certainly never mean, but neither was she light and fluffy and whateverish. But what were their alternatives? Maybe Charlie would answer. Not likely, since he was upstairs. Oh, well.

She pushed the button.

Many bird bones are hollow, saving weight,
yet they have dozens of braces to strengthen them.

—*National Audubon Society First Field Guide: Birds*

CHAPTER

Ten

Ellen was there almost instantly, wearing green sweats for pajamas, her silvery hair disheveled. She let them in silently, a question in her eyes at their own state of disarray. "All right," she said, as they entered. "I trust you have an explanation. Don't you usually go up and down from the trellis?"

Linnet almost fell through the floor. Ellen knew of their expeditions? But there wasn't time for that now. "There are people out there, reporters, waiting to take pictures."

Andy broke in. "It was the ads. They think there are winged people out here."

Ellen closed her eyes. "I knew someone would show up someday. I suppose it's a good thing you two were out gallivanting around."

It all seemed rather anticlimactic, after the long, dark trip and the fear and worry. Linnet felt tears swimming in back of her eyes. The scratch on her cheek started hurting.

"Clean up and go to bed," said Ellen briskly. "And don't turn on any lights in the hallway or your rooms until you have the windows shut and shades down." She went into the kitchen, talking under her breath. "I'll have to tell Charlie and Jan before they get up—only Jake and I can be seen."

Andy started limping toward the stairs, looking as deflated as Linnet felt. Linnet ran to catch up so Andy could lean on her going up. They went along the dark hallway into Andy's room, closing the window and pulling the shade tight to the sash. Andy flopped down on her bed.

Linnet hesitated. Wasn't Andy going to come help shut Linnet's window? Apparently not, and Linnet felt stupid asking. "Well, good night," she said slowly.

"Yeah, yeah, good night, pardner," said Andy. "Sweet dreams, O winged menace to society."

That buoyed Linnet's spirits enough to get her into her own dark bedroom, even though approaching the open window made her feel creepy. There was no way they could see her, though, even if they were awake, and from what she'd heard, she bet they were both sound asleep, dreaming of room service. She cranked the window shut and pulled down the shade as quietly as possible.

She still didn't feel comfortable turning on the lights, so she felt her way down the hall to the bathroom. With the door safely closed, she flipped the switch up and took a closer look at the scratch.

Her reflection didn't tell her anything she didn't already know: her hair was messy, with twigs stuck in it, and her face looked tired as well as scratched. She washed it off carefully, wincing. The house didn't seem so safe anymore.

Tears dripped out, making her look even more babyish. Like someone who needed her mother around.

The next morning, when Linnet woke up, there was a sign that said, CAUTION, LURKING REPORTERS! taped to her shade. As if she could have forgotten. She got dressed and knocked on Andy's door.

"Go away," said a grumpy voice. Linnet sighed. Andy wasn't exactly a morning person, but she could have made an exception today. Oh, well, by the sounds of it, there was someone in the kitchen. She headed down, peeking around the corner to make sure the curtain was drawn across the window before she went in. Jan had made the curtains from bright, vegetable-print fabric, heavy on carrot orange and eggplant purple, but not neglecting the various greens of broccoli and lettuce and watermelon. Having the curtains closed made it a cheery kitchen that could have been any-where, without the view of the Crazy Mountains framed over the sink to remind her of night treks and lurking reporters. Linnet's spirits lifted a bit.

Then she saw Charlie at the stove, and they rose higher. "Hey, kiddo," he said. "In the mood for huckleberry pancakes?"

"Sure," she said. She nodded toward the window. "Did Ellen tell you?"

Charlie poured batter in neat pools on the griddle. "Yes. The jerks. Why can't they go bother the Loch Ness Monster or something?" He leaned toward the sink and spoke into the drain. "Sorry, Nessie, I didn't mean it."

"I don't think she heard you," said Linnet.

"Sure she did. All water is mystically connected." He flipped the pancakes neatly. "Get the syrup, please."

Linnet got it, as well as the sugar, in case Jake was up. He always put sugar on his pancakes instead of syrup. Which, since he was such a messy eater, everyone encouraged. It was a lot easier to clean up grains of sugar than smears of sticky syrup.

By the time the pancakes were done, all the winged members of the group were at the table. Even Andy had hobbled down, looking cross. "Where's Ellen?" she demanded, taking one pancake from the heaping platter in the center of the table.

"Outside," said Jan. "She and Jake are on a combination espionage slash 'Let's look normal' maneuver. We want the reporters bored stiff, mosquito-bit, and out of here."

"To mosquitoes!" Charlie raised a cup of tea.

The mere mention of mosquitoes made Linnet itch. She forked a couple of pancakes onto her plate and doused them in syrup. Let Andy nibble dry pancakes; she was going for the sweet stuff. Just as she was taking a bite, the front door rattled.

Everyone froze, but it was just Ellen, unlocking the door with the key. Jake bounded in. "I saw the bad guys," he said.

Ellen shook her head as she came into the kitchen. "I hope they leave soon, because they couldn't have picked a better spot to watch from. City people they might be, but they are obviously professional journalists. You guys are going to get sick of hanging around in here."

"Hands, Jake," said his mother, as he reached for the pancakes. He sighed and went to the sink to wash up.

Ellen poured herself a cup of coffee.

"Hands, Grammy!" said Jake.

Everyone laughed, including Ellen, who obediently washed her hands. "So," she said briskly, "what's everyone going to do today?"

"Practice flying," said Andy. "Right, Linnet?"

"Yeah, I guess," said Linnet. She was getting tired of it, tired of failing to fly again and again. How had Andy kept this up for so long?

"That's a good idea." Ellen looked around the table. "How about the rest of you?"

"Play," said Jake. "And have Mom read to me."

Jan gave him a look. "Read what?"

Jake put on an angelic grin. "*Winnie-the-Pooh*."

"Ah, come on, Jake. We just read it twice in a row. Can't we read something else? *Charlotte's Web*? *Bambi*? *Lady Chatterley's Lover*?"

"Lady what?"

"Never mind—just not *Winnie-the-Pooh*."

"*Winnie-the-Pooh*," said Jake stubbornly.

"I'll read it to him," said Linnet. She had never read *Winnie-the-Pooh*, although she had vague memories of her mother reading it to her when she was very, very little.

"I thought we were flying," said Andy, sounding put out.

"*Trying* to fly," said Linnet. "We can't do that all day."

Andy bit into her second pancake with a glare.

"Yay, hurray," said Jake. "Do you do voices?"

"Voices?" repeated Linnet doubtfully.

"Yeah," said Jake, "like Eeyore talks like 'Oh, what a gloomy day,' and Roo says 'Shall we eat our sandwiches, Tigger?' and stuff like that." He made Eeyore's voice very low and mournful and Roo's almost unbearably squeaky.

"I don't know," said Linnet. "I think I just read regular."

Jake sighed. "Well, that's better than nothing."

"I'm going to do some reading myself," said Charlie. "And make bread."

Everyone cheered, even Andy. Charlie's bread was about the only thing she didn't skimp on.

"And cinnamon rolls?" begged Linnet. "Please?"

Charlie looked up at the ceiling. "And cinnamon rolls. Why don't I just throw in dough gobs, too."

Ellen perked up. "Will you? We haven't had those for a long time."

"Maybe I won't be doing any reading," said Charlie. "I'll be slaving over a hot stove all day, making bread and cinnamon rolls and dough gobs. Then I'll probably have to make soup to go with the bread. Or maybe a roast."

"We should have bad guys come more often," said Jake. "Cinnamon rolls and Winnie-the-Pooh."

Linnet scraped some of the leftover syrup with her fork and tried to get it to her mouth before most of it oozed between the tines and dripped back onto her plate. She was semisuccessful.

"Jan?" said Ellen. "We haven't heard your plans."

"Yours either." Jan took a sip of coffee. "Okay, I'm going to read something other than you know what—thank you, Linnet. And probably help Charlie out a little. And not practice flying. And—who knows after that."

"I," said Ellen, "am going to putter around in the back yard and look disgustingly normal and wingless and pray for rain. And then I'm going to work in the darkroom."

"Is it supposed to rain?" asked Jan. "I didn't listen to the radio this morning."

"Radio," said Andy. "Yeah, right. One staticky station that plays bad music."

Ellen ignored her. "There's a chance of afternoon showers."

"That ought to dampen their enthusiasm, not to mention their equipment," said Jan. "Maybe they'll leave early."

"Do we still get cinnamon rolls?" asked Jake.

Charlie gave him a smile. "Even if all the bad guys leave the state, I'll still make cinnamon rolls today. Deal?"

"Deal." Jake stuck out a sugary hand, and Charlie shook it, hesitating only a second.

"Come on, Linnet," said Andy. She stood up and winced.

"Come up with another plan," said Ellen. "You can't fly with that ankle."

"You don't fly with your ankles," said Andy.

"No, but there is such a thing as landing—unless you've gotten a lot better without telling me."

Andy turned around and stalked off, the effect ruined somewhat by her limp. A moment later, her bedroom door slammed. Hard.

"I bet that set her mobile fluttering," said Jan. "Do you want to start reading that book now?"

"Okay," said Linnet. "Let's clear off, Jake." They put their sticky plates in the dishwasher.

"Hands, Jake," said Ellen.

When his hands were clean, Jake led Linnet into the living room and picked *Winnie-the-Pooh* off the bookshelf.

They settled onto the couch, and Linnet opened the book. The introduction was a little confusing, but just as she was ready to give up, the story started. Jake snuggled up beside her.

She hadn't remembered the pictures. Every time she turned a page, she had to stop and look for a minute, until Jake nudged her. She particularly liked the one that showed Christopher Robin opening his door in the trunk of a big tree.

Jake chimed in with her on the part where Pooh was telling Christopher Robin to march around with the umbrella and say "Tut, tut, it looks like rain." Linnet laughed and gave the little boy a hug. Then she turned to page twenty: Christopher Robin's legs sticking out from under an umbrella. And on the next page, Winnie-the-Pooh himself, hanging from a balloon.

Linnet stared at the fat little bear hanging beneath the balloon—floating, flying.

That was it. Helium. Helium to make them lighter so their wings didn't have to work so hard.

Fame is a bee.
It has a song—
It has a sting—
Ah, too, it has a wing.

—Emily Dickinson

CHAPTER
Eleven

Linnet jumped up, still holding the book. "I can't read any more right now."

"Hey…" Jake began, but she was running, hoping Ellen wasn't outside, unreachable. She couldn't even call out the door, because then the journalists would know there was someone else in the house and might wonder why only Ellen and Jake went outside. Charlie was at the table, with his arms powdered completely white, kneading a massive lump of dough. "Is Ellen here?" Linnet asked.

He shook his head. "Haven't seen her for a little while. She might be in her room."

She wasn't. Jan was in hers, reading a mystery novel. She just shook her head when Linnet asked about Ellen, apparently unwilling to come completely out of the world of her book.

Linnet went back through the kitchen and upstairs, not really thinking Ellen would be there. But she was, standing outside Andy's door with an indecisive look on her face, as if she didn't know whether she should knock.

Linnet waved the book. "Ellen," she said. "I know how to fly. I know how to fly. See." She shoved the book into Ellen's hands and stabbed the picture with her finger. "See."

Ellen just stood there for a long moment. "Oh," she said. "You are such a clever little bird." She raised her head and looked right at Linnet. "Am I ever glad that Jan was tired of reading *Winnie-the-Pooh*."

Andy's door opened. "Did you call me?" she demanded, obviously trying to sound cross and not at all curious.

Ellen just raised an eyebrow, but Linnet danced around. "We can fly! We can fly! Like Winnie-the-Pooh with a balloon."

As soon as she understood, Andy was dancing around, too, hopping awkwardly on one foot, using her wings for balance.

Ellen retreated. "I'm getting out of here before you winged wonders knock me over. I'll have to go to town for some helium anyway."

The girls danced around a bit longer, their wings hitting the walls and each other. Then Andy banged her foot on the door frame. "Ouch," she said, stopping to bend over and rub her sore ankle.

"I'm sorry," said Linnet.

"You didn't do it—yes, you did, getting me all excited like that. Apology accepted."

They went slowly downstairs. Ellen had obviously just told Charlie, because he was a flour-covered statue, the lump of dough forgotten in front of him. "Maybe even I could fly," he whispered. His twisted wings flared out; usually he kept them folded against his back.

Linnet felt a little sick. Who had done that to him? His wings were covered with fine white feathers, but they were awful parodies of his straight athletic form.

Andy shifted beside her. "Yeah, probably," she said. "We better go tell Jan, too."

Jake was still on the couch, looking mad. "You left," he said. "Why did Grammy take the book?"

"We're going to fly—to try to fly like Pooh. With a balloon. You gave me the idea."

He brightened up. "Really? With a balloon?" His expression turned thoughtful. "But Pooh doesn't have wings. Won't the string get in the way of the wings?"

The girls looked at each other and groaned. "He's right," said Linnet.

"Maybe not," Andy argued. "After all, we can hold on to the glider handle. The cable runs right between our wings when we're flying."

"Yeah," said Linnet slowly. "Maybe." She made a face. "I guess it really won't look like we're flying if we're hanging from balloons."

"Do you want to look like you're flying, or do you want to fly?" asked Andy.

"Fly," said Linnet. "But . . ."

"But it would be nice to look like it, too," said Andy.

"I could be Christopher Robin," said Jake. "Until my wings grow. I could walk around with an umbrella and say 'Tut, tut, it looks like rain.'"

They stared at him for a moment and then exploded into laughter. Linnet's sides started hurting. She tried to settle down, but Andy's expression, laughter stretching her face, set her off again—which made Andy laugh even harder.

They were still gasping with hilarity, Jake looking on with a faintly offended expression, when Jan came into the living room. "So you came up with an idea. I hope it works."

That stopped them. "What do you mean?" asked Linnet, hoarse with laughing.

"Well," said Jan slowly, "it takes a lot of helium to lift someone. Did you ever see one of those balloon sellers float away? And they hold a whole bunch of helium balloons."

Linnet saw the disappointed expression transform Andy's face, felt her own features drop in a similar way. "You mean—"

"I mean that it's a good idea and something to try for, but we shouldn't count on it before we get the bugs worked out. In any case, it probably wouldn't work for Charlie or me. Maybe Andy. You probably have the best chance."

Andy started to stalk off toward the barn, hampered again by her ankle.

"Sorry," Jan murmured. "That was dumb of me. I think I'd better go to my room and take a nap. As punishment." She yawned and left.

This time, Linnet didn't let Andy go alone. She ran and caught up. "It *will* work," she said. "We'll make it work. Even if we have to use a thousand balloons."

Andy tried to get away, but Linnet stubbornly kept to her pace. In a second, she gave up and slowed down. "My stupid mother," Andy said. "She used to play basketball in high school. She's pretty tall. But can you imagine playing basketball with wings?"

They were in the walkway now. "Basketball with wings?" Linnet didn't know what else to say, whether she should be serious or make a joke. She looked at Andy from the corner of her eye. "Uh, maybe no one would notice the wings."

"Good point," said Andy, half a grin creeping up. "After all, basketball jerseys *do* cover a lot."

"Except you'd have to cut the back out," said Linnet. "Maybe they would notice after all."

"Yeah," said Andy, "and I'd foul half the team just running down the court. There goes my basketball career." Her insubstantial grin wavered further.

Linnet dropped the humor entirely. She'd thought about

being stuck here all summer and maybe staying for the school year, but she hadn't gotten as far as thinking about college and an actual career and her whole life. She started feeling sick.

"I know," whispered Andy. "Welcome to the teeny tiny world of the winged."

"What are we going to do? We can't stay here forever."

"We could," said Andy slowly. "I've talked about it with Ellen. Take correspondence courses or e-mail or something. Get some sort of job where we can work from home. Hope that Ellen tracks down some cute boys of the right ages who will fall madly in love with us."

Linnet made a face. "Get real."

"I am," said Andy. She spread her beautiful, dark wings. "Don't I look real? A real freak." She flung herself down on the landing mat.

"You look like a swan," said Linnet. "A black swan. You know, like a ballerina."

"Good plan," said Andy sarcastically. "In my off-season from the basketball team, I could dance ballet. Right."

"I didn't say you should *be* a ballerina," said Linnet, stung. "I said you looked like a swan. Go join a zoo or something."

To her surprise, Andy laughed. "I can just see my job application: Fond of stale bread. Enjoyed ponds as a small child..." Her light mood twisted again, and she looked wistful. "There were swans at the zoo in Omaha. My mom took me once. I loved the otters."

Linnet sat down beside her. "My mother hated zoos. She said they were awful for the animals—to be there just to be stared at."

They both just sat for a while, understanding now exactly why Linnet's mother didn't like zoos.

"Sometimes I think it would be better if everyone knew about us," said Andy. She drew invisible circles on the floor with her finger. "Then we wouldn't have to hide anymore." She looked up at Linnet with a guarded expression. "What do you think?"

Somehow, Linnet could tell that this was an important question. She had to say the right thing, but she didn't know what that was. "What do you mean?"

"Would it be so bad if the reporters found out about us? And then we could just get on with our lives. Maybe it wouldn't be so bad."

A quiver ran up between Linnet's wings. "You mean going out? While they're here? Ellen would kill us."

Andy flared up. "Ellen is an old lady with no wings who doesn't have to hide anywhere."

"She lets us stay here. Her own daughter and—"

"I know, I know," said Andy. "I don't think I'd really do it. But I can't stand to think of hiding out my whole life. Someday I'm just going to have to get out. I can just see it—'Girls with wings on the next *Oprah* equivalent.' Want to be on TV with me?"

Linnet shrugged. She didn't want to think about it any-more—people finding out, not finding out, having to stay here, being a curiosity. And where did her mother fit in—if she ever turned up again?

Linnet turned away from the thoughts. "What happened to Charlie's wings? Do you know?"

"Not really. It's not exactly the type of thing you can ask someone: so, how did you end up horribly mutilated?"

They were quiet for several minutes. Then Andy said, "This is terrible. We have to do something, or I'm going to go crazy."

"What?"

"You practice your flying," she ordered. "Since I can't."

Linnet ran to the other end of the barn and climbed onto the platform. This was right. She had to move. She grabbed the handle, started flapping, and jumped—and just about creamed Andy at the other end.

"Not bad," said Andy, from the floor where she'd rolled to get out of the way. "Except you're not supposed to aim for your coach."

"Some coach," said Linnet. "Lying around on the land-ing field." The big, bad future disappeared. She went back for another almost-flight. It was so close. She could almost convince herself that she felt lift along with momentum.

Then a thought hit her, as she was whizzing toward the mat. Her concentration broke, and she let go a second too late and smacked into the wall.

"Are you okay?" Andy asked, dropping to her knees beside her.

Linnet brushed the question aside. "We don't need as much help," she said, rubbing her head. "We're almost there."

"Huh? Linnet? Are you seeing double? How many fingers am I holding up?"

"No, I'm okay. I mean about the balloons, why the balloon sellers don't float away. We almost fly the way it is, with no balloons. It shouldn't take much to really get us going."

"Girl, you are brilliant."

Linnet stood up and bowed. "Thank you. Thank you very much."

Ellen came into the barn with a list in her hand. "I'm going to go into town for some helium and something to put it in. The more I think about this, the more I doubt it's going to work. But it's the only idea anyone's had in a while, so it's definitely worth a try." She shrugged. "Can't hurt. Do either of you want anything else from town?"

"Boys," said Andy.

Ellen raised her eyebrows and poised her pen, but Linnet thought she saw serious sympathy mixed in with the mockery. "With or without wings?"

"Either."

Ellen scribbled on the list. "You, Linnet? Boys? Or anything else?"

"I don't know," said Linnet. The only thing she could think of—besides the flying stuff—was her mother, and she couldn't exactly put her on a shopping list.

"Okay, then," said Ellen. "Helium, balloons, and boys. Your basic ordinary list. I shouldn't be long."

Linnet made a couple more flights after Ellen left, but she could tell that Andy was just itching to fly, sore ankle or not. "Let's go see if Charlie will give us some dough," she said, as Andy was eyeing the launching platform speculatively.

"Okay," said Andy, her voice reluctant.

The glass bricks in the tunnel glowed with diffused sunshine. If it was going to rain, it sure didn't look like it. Linnet sighed. It would have been the perfect day to be outside, and they had to waste it in here, waiting for the reporters to go away. Worse yet, it was so glorious that the reporters would undoubtedly be in no hurry to go anywhere. Summer days in the mountains, with the aspens vivid against the darker green of the pines, firs, and spruces—nothing was more wonderful.

"When do you think they'll leave?" she asked.

Andy shrugged, her wings fluttering with the movement. "Pretty soon, probably. As long as they don't see anything interesting."

Linnet didn't like the way Andy tossed her head when she said that. Even without wings, a tall, dark girl with red-gold hair and a prickly personality was interesting. Add the wings and Andy could get interviewed by anyone she wanted. Late-night talk shows. Prime-time news. Any magazine in the country. Or all of the above.

"Can you imagine the story they'd write if they knew about us?" Linnet exaggerated her voice and made up a few more headlines. "FREAKS THAT FLY. MUTANTS IN MONTANA. WINGED WEIRDOS."

Andy pushed her. "Watch who you're calling a winged weirdo, winged weirdo."

An hour later, the walkway between the barn and the house was oddly dark. The glass bricks seemed like leaden squares that actually sucked the light out. "If we could look out the windows," said Andy, "I bet we'd see a real storm brewing. It's kind of fun to be out in a storm with wings— as long as it isn't too cold. You blow around as fast as you can run, sometimes faster. And rain on your bare wings..." She shivered. "It's awesome. With these idiot reporters here, though, I guess you can't try it this time. Maybe it'll chase 'em away."

"I hope so," said Linnet, even though she wasn't sure about being out in a storm. It sounded frightening. But then, midnight trips to stargaze on the rocks were frightening, too, and she wouldn't give up that experience for anything. That was one good thing about having Andy for a friend: nothing was boring.

They meandered through the living room and into the kitchen again. Charlie had come out of his earlier daze and was back to work on the bread. He gave them each another blob of dough. Linnet ate hers immediately, but Andy twisted hers into odd shapes. "Can I have another piece?" she asked, when she'd finally eaten it.

"Don't you guys have somewhere to go?" asked Charlie. "Hint, hint."

"Awww, Charlie doesn't like us anymore," said Andy.

"I've changed my mind. You can stay and help me with the dishes."

"We're going," Linnet said hastily. "Right, Andy?"

"When you're right, you're right."

They headed out of the kitchen. Charlie called after them, "Okay, if you insist—you can do the dishes later."

They were halfway up the stairs when the doorbell rang.

"I can't come," she said apologetically, "I have forgotten how to fly."

—*J. M. Barrie*, Peter Pan

CHAPTER

Twelve

Linnet started to run down, but Andy grabbed her. "Are you an idiot? You can't answer the door."

Linnet shook her off. "I know that. I'm going to find Jake. Get in your room." She gave Andy a gentle push and ran back to the kitchen.

Charlie's face was white as the flour on the table. "Don't answer it," he whispered.

But Linnet couldn't bear not knowing who was out there. "Where's Jake?" she asked. "He could check. He doesn't have wings yet."

"I don't think we should let a little kid answer the door alone," said Charlie.

"He won't really be alone," said Linnet. The doorbell rang again, longer this time. "Where is he? You should go hide."

"In his room, I think." Charlie shook excess flour from his hands. "I'll open the pantry door and stand behind it—that way no one can see me, but I'll still be right here if Jake needs me."

"Good idea," said Linnet. She ran through the living room. The doorbell sounded again. "Jake," she called, trying to keep her voice low so whoever was out there couldn't hear. "Jake! Come here—I've got a mission for you."

Jake looked out into the hall. "What?" he asked.

The doorbell, and a knock. They were probably about to go away. Linnet's words rushed out. "Go answer the door and tell them your mom is in the shower. Just see who it is and tell them to come back later. Can you do that?"

Jake narrowed his eyes. "Of course I can," he said. "But my mom's not taking a shower. She's taking a nap. That would be lying."

"It would be more like pretending," Linnet said. "Like Christopher Robin saying 'Tut, tut, it looks like rain' for Winnie-the-Pooh. Right?" Just as she was convincing him, it occurred to her that he could have just as easily used the nap excuse, but it didn't make any difference now.

Jake grinned. "Right. Okay."

"Hurry," Linnet said. There was more knocking, but she was afraid their visitor was about to leave.

Jake ran for the door, singing, "Mommy's in the shower. Mommy's in the shower."

Linnet followed him as far as the living room. She crouched behind the couch, furling her wings tightly. By peeking through the leaves of the big plant beside the couch, she could remain hidden and still see the door.

Jake fumbled with the lock. "In the shower, in the shower," he sang softly. He opened the door. "Hello," he called, into a swirl of strong wind.

Obviously, the person had given up and started to walk away. "I thought no one was home," said a soft voice.

Jake went into his spiel. "My mom's in the shower. You can come back—"

That was as far as he got. Linnet leaped up and ran to the open door. "Mother," she said, stopping, suddenly self-conscious about the great wings she had grown over the summer. She folded them as tightly as she could, but the wind pressed against them and they flared out again.

Her mother's eyes were large in her pale face. "Oh, Linnet," she said. "I'm sorry. There was a mix-up. I couldn't..."

Within Linnet, anger fought with relief. No words would come out, but a flood of tears threatened to wash her away. "I hate you!" she shouted, and ran for the stairs, banging a wingtip painfully on the banister.

She gave the door to her room a slam that Andy would have been proud of. Thunder grumbled outside. "I hate her, I hate her, I hate her," she muttered, storming about. It was true, but it wasn't. She'd never been so glad to see anyone in her life. And what if she left now, because Linnet had yelled? She wouldn't, would she?

Andy's door opened and shut, quietly. Linnet waited a few minutes, long enough for Andy to hobble down the stairs, and slipped into the hallway. Ordinary conversation sounds filtered up, interspersed with the growing storm outside. Rain lashed against the window, making it hard to hear what was going on below. Was her mother still there? She stole closer to the stairs. Yes, the quiet voice was part of it, but she couldn't tell what anyone was saying. Keeping her wings in, she crept down, a step at a time, silent as smoke.

"... really ticked because you dumped her," Andy was saying.

"What? Huh?" That was Charlie.

Jake's voice. "You dumped her out? Why?" No one responded to him.

"And because you left her with the grandma who cuts off wings."

Charlie made some incoherent sound, and Jake said, "Grandmas don't cut off wings. Do they?"

Linnet found she was clutching the railing so hard her hand hurt. There was silence now. What would her mother say? What could she say?

"But she wanted to go there," her mother cried. "She asked to. And I didn't leave her with my mother; I left her at the motel. I was going to take her over there, but when we got to Livingston, I just couldn't, I couldn't...I tried to find out and—and..."

The words dissolved into the sound of her mother crying. Linnet couldn't stand it. She ran into the kitchen and found herself hugging her untouchable mother—and being hugged back. "I'm so sorry," her mother sobbed. "I'm so sorry."

"You didn't come back," said Linnet. "I didn't know what to do, and Margaret brought me here." A thought hit her, and she pulled back. "How did you find me?"

The sobs died down. "I didn't mean to leave you at all," Sarah said. "I just wanted to see her, watch her from a distance, decide if it was okay."

Her face was pinched. "I was parked in front of her house, watching it, about five A.M., when a police car pulled up behind me. I got scared and took off, and they chased me and took me in and held me."

This was not at all what Linnet had expected to hear. The others were standing around, frozen, even Jake, just listening. Sarah didn't seem to notice them.

"Why didn't you call me?" asked Linnet. "I was so scared."

"I couldn't call you. They would have found out about you. I just kept telling them they'd scared me and I shouldn't have run and I was sorry. Finally, they let me go. When I got to the motel, you were gone."

"I left you a note," Linnet cried.

Sarah shrugged. "There was no note. Maybe the maid took it when she was cleaning up. Anyway, I didn't know where you'd gone. I couldn't call the police. I thought maybe you'd tried to go home. But I didn't think you had money. I was hoping that you hadn't tried hitchhiking or that you hadn't been abducted." Her eyes glittered with tears. "So, after a week, I went home. But you weren't there. I hoped you'd come soon." Charlie handed her a box of tissues, which she took gratefully.

She blew her nose. "Since I'd never told you your grandmother's name, I didn't think you could have gone to her. How did you know where to go?"

"The messages in the garbage," said Linnet. She was oddly calm now, as if this were all some mystery book they'd read different parts of. "I could read her name—it wasn't crossed out all the way."

Sarah tried to smile. "So I guess I did write you a note after all. I couldn't think of what to say, so I was just going to try to get back before you woke up."

She went on. "After I'd been home a while and you hadn't come, I was desperate."

"But I tried to call," said Linnet. "And then the phone was disconnected. I called the motel, too."

Sarah hugged her again. "They shut the phone off when

I was in Livingston—I forgot to pay the bill before we left. When I got back, I got it turned back on. You must have called the motel after I checked out. I'm so sorry." She gave Linnet another hug.

"And I tried to call you at work, but this woman said she'd never heard of you."

"She's new," said Sarah. "Hired a couple of days after we left for Montana."

"That still doesn't get us to where you found this place," said Andy.

Sarah jumped, fully aware of the audience again.

"Why don't you sit down," said Charlie. "I'll make you a cup of tea, if you'd like." He didn't wait for her to answer but turned to fill the teakettle at the sink, his wings held stiffly.

Sarah sat down, and Linnet pulled out a chair next to her. "I decided I had to go back to Livingston and see if I could find you. My boss"—she made a face—"wasn't too pleased, but I went back. I stayed in the same motel, but there didn't seem to be anything to do to find you. I don't know what I was thinking." She closed her eyes. "And then I decided to talk to my mother. I had no idea you had gone to her, but I couldn't think of anything else to do."

Jan wandered into the kitchen at this point, yawning and stretching. She stopped dead at the sight of the stranger, looking from her to Linnet and back again. "I don't need to ask who you are," she said. "I'm Jan."

"She's my mom," Jake explained. "And Ellen's my grandma. Not the kind of grandma who cuts off wings."

Jan started to say something, but a look from Charlie stopped her. "So should we call you 'Linnet's mother'?"

"Her name is Sarah," said Charlie, just as she said, "My name is Sarah." They both blushed.

Jan grinned. "Well, Sarah, I know that Ellen would say you're more than welcome to stay here, as long as you're willing to pitch in. Frankly, we could use another adult who can go out in public."

"Oh, no, we couldn't..." Sarah's words died off in midsentence.

"How would you hide Linnet's wings?" Jan spoke softly.

There was a long moment of silence. "I'd have to go get our stuff." Sarah's voice was shaky.

Somewhere in the midst of the discussion, Andy disappeared. Linnet didn't notice exactly when. When she did, something twinged inside her. "I'm going to check on something," she said.

Andy wasn't in her room. Were the shades slightly askew? Linnet couldn't be sure. She clattered down the stairs and raced through the house and into the barn.

Andy was sitting on the launching platform, one foot dangling off, the other knee hugged to her chest. "Hi," said Linnet, feeling stupid.

The other girl didn't respond.

Linnet climbed up. "Your ankle must be killing you," she said.

"It's not."

"Oh." Now what? "Uh, do you want to coach me on a takeoff?"

Andy turned a smoldering gaze on her. "You want everything, don't you? Now you've got your beloved little mother and you're going to be able to fly because of your brilliant idea and you want my help. Forget it."

"But you'll be able to fly, too," said Linnet. "I—"

"How the hell do you know?" Andy cried. "How much do you weigh? Sixty pounds? Practically nothing. I am so damn tall that I can't get below ninety and still be strong. How do you know that I'll be able to fly?"

"You will," Linnet said fiercely. "We'll just add the right amount of helium until you can. You have to fly."

Andy burst into tears. "If I can't, though—oh, why did I grow wings? They're spoiling my life. What good are they?"

Linnet patted her shoulder awkwardly. "It'll be okay," she whispered. "Really."

"I almost believe you," said Andy. "Almost." She wiped the tears from her cheeks with long, dark fingers. "I need to be by myself."

"Okay," said Linnet. She grabbed the handle and jumped, not even flapping. The rush of air caught her spread wings, and she glided to the end and let go.

"We *will* fly," she said, landing with a few running steps. "We will."

Her mother was alone in the living room, looking at the photographs. It seemed so strange to see her here. *Probably not nearly as strange as it seems for her to see me with these wings, though,* Linnet thought. "Hi, Mom," she said.

"Linnet." Her mother looked uncomfortable. "Do you want to stay here? Because if you don't, we'll work something else out..." The way her voice trailed away on the last sentence, it was clear she had no idea what that something else might be.

"I like it here," Linnet said. "If you do."

"What would I do? I can't exactly work in a photocopying place from here."

Linnet shrugged. "I don't know. Help with the shopping and stuff? A lot of times Ellen has to stop working on whatever she's doing just to go to town." The conversation was making her cross. A kid wasn't supposed to have to tell her mother how to run her life. "I don't care what you do."

Before they could say anything else, the doorbell rang again.

However, in a storm they fly much closer to the ground
so that they can take refuge quickly in an emergency.

—*Pierre Gingras,* The Secret Lives of Birds

CHAPTER

Thirteen

Jan and Charlie and Jake appeared almost instantly. "Now what?" Jan hissed, although she could have spoken loudly amid the sounds of the storm.

"It's too early for Ellen to be back from town," said Charlie. "And even if she was, she'd just let herself in." Since ringing doorbells were a major problem when there were no unwinged adults in the house, Ellen never used theirs.

Again it rang, almost simultaneously with a crash of thunder.

"It must be the reporters," said Linnet, just as Andy limped in. The doorbell sounded in the barn, too—not so someone there could come answer it, but as a warning to stay inside.

"We can't just leave them out there in this," said Jan, as

lightning flared brightly enough to be visible through the curtains.

"We can, too," said Andy. "They're not supposed to be here anyway."

"Lightning storms in the mountains are very dangerous. They could get killed."

"Serve them right," said Andy, but she didn't look as if she really meant it.

Linnet didn't know what to think. "Maybe we could hide," she said. "And they wouldn't know anyone was home."

Jan shook her head. "Too late. They can see that there are lights on even though the curtains are closed."

"And my car is parked right out in front," said Sarah.

Jake had latched on to Linnet's idea. "Yeah, let's hide in Grammy's darkroom. It would be fun. Even if they came in the house, they couldn't find us, because we'd turn the don't-come-in light on."

"That," said Jan, "is an excellent idea. Those of us with wings—and Jake—will hide in the darkroom." She turned to Sarah. "I'm sorry to have to get you in the thick of this when you've just arrived, but you'll have to let them in and entertain them for the remainder of the storm. And then politely—and quickly—get rid of them."

Sarah gulped. "Okay," she said. "But what can I tell them? What is this place supposed to be?"

"You'll think of something. Hurry now," Jan said, herding

the others ahead of her like a flock of geese. "Wait until you hear a door close, and then you can let them in," she called back to Sarah. "Show them around a little, maybe— everywhere except the darkroom."

Linnet felt odd about leaving her mother alone to face the reporters, but proud at the same time. It seemed to take forever to get all of them arranged in the small darkroom, their wings brushing against each other and against the smooth jugs of chemicals. Finally, Charlie closed the door, locked it, and flipped the switch that turned on the outside warning light. Unfortunately, that also shut off the regular overhead light. In the dim amber, the wings looked frightening.

"This is not going to be fun," said Andy, twisting around. Her wings bumped Linnet's.

"It is, too," said Jake. "It's like hide-and-seek." His voice sounded a bit shrill, though.

"Of course it's going to be fun," said Jan. It was hard to tell in the near dark, but Linnet thought she shot a glare at Andy. "And you're the luckiest one, because you're little enough to lie down under the bench and have your own place, even more secret than the rest of us."

Jake fell for it and crawled under immediately. "Cool," he cried, his voice echoing oddly in the small room.

"Actually, I was thinking a bit warm," said Andy.

Linnet agreed; five people in a darkroom meant for one or two was going to be warm and stuffy soon.

Her eyes were fully adjusted now, and she could see the strips of negatives hanging from clips, the boxy shape of the enlarger. Too bad it was so crowded, or they could develop some pict—

She gasped.

"What?" said Jan.

"The picture. Of Andy. Lying on her rock with her wings spread out. It's in my room."

"They won't go upstairs," said Charlie. "Will they?"

"They'd better not," muttered Jan. Andy was silent for a change.

"Sssh," said Charlie, who was nearest the door.

Sarah's voice, speaking artificially loud. "You can't go in there; that's the darkroom. I'll show you the . . . barn next."

"What a lovely camp," said one of the reporters, the man. "Can you show us the sleeping accommodations? We might want to stay sometime."

"That wouldn't—I suppose . . ." Sarah sounded uncertain.

"I love the photographs," said the woman. "So . . ." The voices trailed off.

"Well, that's it, then," said Andy. "They're going to see the picture." Did she sound just the slightest bit excited?

"No," said Linnet, squeezing past Andy and Jan. "Unlock the door, Charlie."

In this world
even butterflies
have to earn their living.

—Issa

CHAPTER

Fourteen

"What are you going to do?" Jan asked softly.

"I'll run upstairs and get the picture while they're in the barn. Then I'll come back."

"What if they get back into the house part while you're still upstairs?" Andy asked. "Then what will you do? Pose?"

"I'll go out my window and climb down the trellis," she said. "Then I can hide in my mother's car until the storm dies down."

"It could work," said Jan. "And you're the only one of us who could do it. We could try sending Jake, but he might not be able to find your picture or hide it reliably. Charlie and I are probably too heavy for the trellis. And Andy's..."

"If I didn't have this stupid sprained ankle," said Andy.

Charlie reached past the light-blocking curtain and unlocked the door.

Linnet stepped past him. The curtain slid across her wing-tips, as if something dark were touching her. She shivered and opened the door, cautiously peeking her head out.

No one in the hallway. "Okay," she said, her voice low. "See you later. I'll scratch on the door when I want to come back in."

She went as quickly and quietly down the hall as she could. She risked a glance into the walkway. Nothing. The living room. Past the kitchen. Up the stairs. Were there sounds? Hard to tell with the storm fury masking mere human noises. She passed Andy's room and slipped into her own.

The picture was above her nightstand, just pinned to the wall with a couple of tacks. Jan was going to show her how to frame it, but she hadn't gotten around to it yet. Just as well, because it would be easier to carry. She slipped it into the front of her shirt. The edges of the photographic paper dug into her skin.

She was just ready to leave her room when the scrap of paper on the shade caught her eye: CAUTION, LURKING REPORTERS! She darted over and snatched it. That would be a dead giveaway.

Linnet didn't bother to listen before racing into Andy's room on light feet. She hadn't bargained on having to go into three rooms. Now speed was way more important than silence.

She grabbed Andy's warning sign and did a quick visual

check. The winged horses were the most incriminating thing, but she didn't have time to deal with them. Down to Charlie's room.

Linnet had never been in Charlie's room. It was similar to hers and Andy's except that he'd taken down the winged mobile, whatever it was. The ceiling looked bare.

So did the shade. No warning sign. She went over to see if it had fallen off. Nothing. Apparently Ellen had only put the notes in her and Andy's rooms, since they were kids. She flicked the light switch off and started out.

A sudden lull in the storm revealed footsteps on the stairs. Linnet backed into Charlie's room and shut the door quietly. Damn. Now what? If she was in her room or Andy's room, she could do the roof thing, but Charlie's room was over the old part of the house. There wasn't a convenient kitchen roof jutting out below his window, with an even more convenient trellis providing a ladder to the ground.

The tiny closet could have held a Linnet without wings, but forget it now. Likewise under the bed. She would have to go out the window anyway. "It will be like flying off the platform," she whispered to herself, tugging the shade up and climbing on top of the dresser. She stuffed the two warning signs down her shirt, barely noticing the added discomfort.

The window latch twisted aside easily. Linnet had half been hoping it would stick.

Charlie's window was the old-fashioned kind that you just pushed up rather than the kind you cranked out. Linnet pushed it up, and the storm hit her. She unhooked the screen and angled it out. Before she could drop it, a gust ripped it from her hands.

She couldn't do this. It would be nothing like going off the platform in the barn. Even as she was thinking this, she was sliding her feet out. The wind slapped her with a handful of cold needles. *Sure, Andy, being out in a storm is a blast.* She wriggled her wings through and the wind caught at them, pushing and pulling, screaming in her ears.

She couldn't wait, or they would come. She couldn't jump, or she would die. She leaned forward just a bit, trying to see the ground better, and the wind took the decision from her.

Do you show the hawk how to fly,
stretching his wings on the wind?

—*Book of Job*

CHAPTER

Fifteen

The window slammed shut behind Linnet. A blast of wind held her against the rough siding for a second and then dropped her. Instinct—or lessons learned in a hundred launches from the platform—took over, and she was flapping, as strong and wild as the storm. Almost.

Cold, dark, erratic. Rain stung Linnet's eyes and made her gasp. A weird uplift took her higher, and for the first time she felt as if she were truly flying. If Andy had felt even a tenth of this running on the ground, faster than she could run, Linnet could understand why she loved it. Then lightning seared the night, thunder cracking before the light had faded. A pine tree loomed into existence directly in front of her.

Linnet would have screamed, but she didn't have time.

Every speck of her energy and concentration went into avoiding the tree. Her previous work in the barn was of little use now, as she hadn't exactly learned how to turn on those straight-line, cable-assisted flights.

Somehow she managed not to hit the tree. The wind she was riding veered past and then, as if it regretted helping her, swirled and dissolved into the cold rain. The sudden loss of lift made her falter and drop.

Another flash showed her the ground.

Too late.

The dove descending breaks the air.

—*T. S. Eliot,* "Little Gidding"

CHAPTER

Sixteen

Linnet hit hard and crooked, her left leg buckling under her in sudden pain. She fell sideways and scraped a wing against a branch as she went down. Wet pine needles dug into her hands as she tried to catch herself, slipped, and landed facedown on the ground.

Dazed, she just lay there, whimpering, trying to figure out how badly she was hurt. The leg was the worst—probably a sprained ankle. She felt her wing and winced.

A sudden gust plastered her with rain. She shivered. A sprained ankle couldn't kill a person. Could being out in a rainstorm? What about hypothermia? Another blast of thunder and lightning made her scream, her voice lost in the storm. Lightning certainly could kill her. Phase two of her plan: she had to get to her mother's car.

Linnet looked around as best she could in the intermittent darkness. Rain lashed her face. She was near the rock where they fed scraps to the animals. The locked back door was only fifty feet away. The wind tore at her wings, and for a cold, wet moment she considered banging on the door, reporters or not.

For a moment. But it wasn't her decision alone. Besides, if she did that now, her sprained ankle and scraped wing would be for nothing.

Walking was not an option, not with her ankle feeling the way it did. She started crawling toward the house. The structure didn't give her much protection, since the storm was coming at her from the wrong angle, but it made her feel slightly safer. She crawled along the house—past the trellis, under Andy's window, around the corner. Her knees and palms felt raw and bruised. She stopped, sobbing, when she made the corner, hoping for more protection. But the wind and rain seemed to be coming from all directions.

At least this was the short side of the house. Not so far to the next corner. And then the gravel driveway. Linnet made herself stop thinking about it. "Just go," she whispered to herself. She was shivering hard now. Cold. Wet. Sore. And the picture—the stupid picture that had caused all this—scratched against her stomach as she crawled along.

Another corner. There was a tiny bit of protection along the front of the house, but it didn't last long because she had to angle out toward the car. Her knees felt like hamburger by now, grinding into the sharp, wet gravel. "Andy owes me a pair of jeans," she hissed. Dumb, she knew, because it wasn't Andy who had taken the picture and left it displayed. Besides, if it weren't for the picture, she wouldn't have removed the warning notes. The reporters—everything was their fault. But she couldn't exactly confront them on the issue: "Because you were snooping around, I trashed my knees and a good pair of jeans and sprained my ankle. Oh, and I scratched my wing, too." Yeah, that would work.

It was good that she was mad. It helped her focus on something besides being miserable. Still, by the time she reached her mother's car, she was a crawling disaster.

Lightning hit again, nearby. Linnet jumped and banged her head on the bumper. She scrambled the last few feet to the door. Reached up.

It was locked.

Even the most winged spirit cannot escape physical necessity.

—*Kahlil Gibran,* Sand and Foam

CHAPTER
Seventeen

Lightning cracked the sky. Linnet was shivering uncontrollably now. If she couldn't get in the car, she would have to crawl up to the front door and demand to be let in. Never mind that the worst possible people would be there, ready to take notes and pictures.

She crawled around to the other side, hoping that the driver's door would be unlocked. No.

When she was little, she was with a friend once when his parents locked their keys in the car. They all scrabbled around with their hands in the bumpers and wheel wells. Linnet was the one to finally find the secret, magnetic box. Did her mother have anything like that?

There didn't seem to be anything in the gritty nooks and crannies. Those little flat boxes were easy to miss, though.

She kept looking. She was crouched at the front of the car when the storm noise changed a little. More of a steady groan.

Then she saw the headlights. Linnet froze for a second. Was this someone coming to look for the reporters? Or Ellen?

She dove for the darkness, outside the swath of light created by the headlights. Even if it was Ellen, her mother and the reporters might notice the approaching car and look out the window. As if her thought had created the reality, she saw a curtain lift, faces peer out. Now what? Linnet flattened herself against the ground and tried to keep her wings down with the wind tugging at them.

The vehicle stopped close to the front door. When the door opened, the interior light illuminated Ellen. She looked puzzled. "Linnet?" she called into the storm, looking around. "Is that you?" Her silver hair slicked and darkened in the rain. "Whose car is this?"

"It's my mom's. And the reporters are here," Linnet yelled out, trusting that the noise from the storm would mask her voice from the people inside. "I can't go in. And the car is locked." Even to herself she sounded hysterical. Weirdly, now that Ellen was here, she felt worse—like a kid who doesn't start crying until Mom or Dad sees her skinned knee.

"Emergency kit. In the back." Ellen didn't say any more.

She dipped her head in what may have been a nod and set about getting groceries out. She started to pick up a second bag and then set it back down. The curtain dropped and a few seconds later, as Ellen approached the house at a run, the door opened.

When it closed, Linnet made her way painfully to Ellen's Jeep and let herself in the back left door.

After being in the storm, the Jeep seemed like a cocoon. Rain drummed on the roof and windshield, a sound Linnet had always loved. Now she loved it more, because it meant there was something between her and cold water.

Except, of course, for the cold water she'd brought in with her. Her clothes were heavy, plastered to her body, her shoes filled with water. She was shivering like an aspen leaf. Ignoring the bags of groceries for the moment, she reached over the back of the seat and started feeling around for the emergency kit. A couple of helpful flashes of lightning— amazing how much more she appreciated the lightning when she was insulated from the ground by four rubber tires—helped in her search.

The emergency kit was a coffee can stuffed with supplies: a small first-aid kit, old candy bars, a plastic bottle of water, a squatty candle, matches in a glass jar, a folded blanket made out of thin silvery material, a flashlight.

Linnet set the flashlight on the seat and pushed the button with a shaking finger. The small, warm circle of light was worth the risk of being seen, she thought. And anyway, Ellen wouldn't let them look out the front windows until they were ready to leave, which wouldn't be until the storm was over. She'd just have to be alert, ready to duck down onto the floor at the first sign of them emerging.

First she had to get warm. The silvery blanket was awkward to open fully in the back seat and seemed too thin to do much good, but almost as soon as she had it tented over her wings, she felt—not warm, but as if warmth were possible.

She looked briefly at the first-aid kit before setting it aside. She doubted there was anything she could do for her ankle, even though it was throbbing and swollen, and she couldn't even reach the scratch on her wing. None of the bandages were big enough for her knees or shaped right for her palms, and she wasn't about to put stinging antiseptic on the already painful scrapes.

Thunder smashed the night again. Was there more of a delay now between light and sound? Not much of one, but perhaps the storm was starting to move off.

Now that the shivers were subsiding, Linnet noticed that she was fiercely hungry. Shielding the flashlight with her hand, she let pink stripes of light fall into the nearest grocery bag. A lot of green beans and corn and peaches; useless out here without a can opener. Toothpaste. Cherry tomatoes. Could you eat those without washing them first?

Lemons for Charlie to cook with. She looked into the next bag.

Much better. The first thing she saw was a rectangular block of sharp Cheddar cheese. She put the flashlight down and ripped the plastic open. Feeling wonderfully barbaric, she bit off a mouthful. "Just let them get mad at me," she muttered, her mouth full.

A couple more bites and she'd had enough cheese. Examining the bag again, she pulled out a box of cereal. Shredded wheat squares, the tiny ones with frosting on them. Dessert!

Cheese and shredded wheat make you thirsty, Linnet decided, rummaging again. Unfortunately, there was nothing to drink in the grocery bags. She went back to the coffee can and pulled out the water bottle. Judging from the condition of the candy bars, this was ancient water, emergency water, probably unfit for human consumption. Now that she was beginning to be warm, she didn't feel quite so desperate. Still . . .

Tilting the bottle in front of the flashlight, Linnet decided to give it a try.

Mistake.

Her taste buds shriveled on her tongue at first contact with what tasted like pure liquid plastic. "Bleah," she sputtered, spitting it out with reflex action. Not that it mattered, since her clothes were far from dry.

All of a sudden, she felt less like the defiant barbarian and more like the miserable girl with shredded knees, crawling for shelter.

Carefully, mindful of all her sore spots, Linnet curled up on the seat, making sure she was completely covered by the silver blanket. A bag of canned goods made a lousy pillow. Putting the cereal box flat on top of it helped some. So the shredded wheat would be smushed and soggy wheat. She couldn't bring herself to care.

There were no comfortable positions. Linnet settled for the least uncomfortable. Every once in a while, white light infiltrated her blanket cocoon. The storm was definitely on its way out.

Just as definitely, it was in no hurry. Rain danced on the Jeep's roof. The rhythmic, hypnotic sound lulled her to sleep.

"I think I'd like to fly," I told the family casually that evening, knowing full well I'd die if I didn't. "Not a bad idea," said my father equally casually. "When do you start?"

—Amelia Earhart, The Fun of It

CHAPTER
Eighteen

The sound of the front door slamming. Linnet remembered in time—just—where she was and what was going on. She tugged the silver blanket back over her head and pulled her feet under, stifling a yelp as she bumped her sore ankle.

The sound of Ellen's voice filtered through the window. "Remember that this is private property. Next time you're out hiking, please stay on public land."

"We're sorry," one of the reporters said, the woman with the scratchy voice. "Thank you for letting us wait out the storm."

Were they going to walk past the Jeep? Was any part of her showing? Linnet tensed every stiff muscle unconsciously.

Crunching of shoes on gravel. Steps coming closer.

Closer. Angling away. They were going around the back of the house, Linnet guessed. Back the way they had come. She let out a breath and then tensed again as steps came directly toward the Jeep. The door opened and the scent of rain-washed air poured in.

"Linnet?"

Her mother's voice. Linnet peeked out from under the blanket. Sarah leaned into the Jeep.

"Are you all right?"

Tears wanted to leak out, but Linnet wouldn't let them. "I sprained my ankle," she said. "But I'm okay. What about the others?"

"Ellen is letting them know the reporters have gone," Sarah said. "Let's get you inside."

Wings were actually an asset where a sprained ankle was concerned. It was easier to balance and put weight on the other foot once they'd figured out the logistics of Linnet leaning on her mother's arm. "I didn't know you were out there," Sarah said. "I wondered what was going on when we came into the farthest upstairs room and there was water on the dresser. I told the reporters that I'd left the window open and it must have blown shut. And then Ellen came in and we had to pretend we knew each other."

Linnet was using all her energy to hobble. The steps were a bit of a trick, and her wings turned into a definite liability when they reached the door. Sarah had to hold on to Linnet's hands and go in backward.

Then the others were crowding around, trying to help. Jan and Charlie picked Linnet up, and she cried out in pain. "My knees," she said. "Careful!"

They set her on the couch.

"What happened?" asked Andy. "Did you fall off the trellis?"

Linnet shook her head. "I had to go out Charlie's window."

"While you're telling the whole story, we'll get you fixed up. These pants look like candidates for cutoffs," said Jan. "I'll get the scissors."

"Did you get the picture?" Andy asked.

Linnet reached into her shirt and pulled out the bent, soggy picture, one corner ripped completely off. It was still striking, something a tabloid reporter would have sold fingers and toes to print. "I got the notes from the shades, too," she said. "That's why I was in Charlie's room."

Ellen looked surprised. "But I didn't put a note in Charlie's room."

"I didn't know that," said Linnet. "So I went in there to check. I was just getting ready to go, and then I heard them coming up the stairs. So I went out the window. The flying was incredible."

There was a burble of comment at that, but Ellen waved everyone silent. "We'll all ask questions later. Let's let Linnet finish the story."

"The flying was scary, but—oh, I can't wait to do it

again. Except not in the middle of a storm."

She paused in her recital to wince as Jan eased the ruined pant leg over her swollen ankle. Sarah wrapped an ice-filled towel around the ankle, and Linnet finished the story. "But how did you guys survive the whole storm crowded in the darkroom?"

"We barely did," Andy said sourly. "You wouldn't believe how stuffy that was."

"Oh, right, I forgot. I was out in the fresh air," said Linnet.

Andy gave her a sheepish grin. "Thanks for going after the evidence."

"Isn't anyone going to ask me about *my* expedition?" said Ellen.

"You got the helium!" cried Linnet and Andy in chorus.

"It's in the front seat of the Jeep, along with balloons and inflatable vests and water wings. You ought to be able to fly by the time we hook you up to all that paraphernalia and fill it with helium."

"Yeah, if you didn't have to land," said Jan dryly, looking at Linnet with her iced ankle and Andy standing on one leg, not putting any weight on her injured one.

"I can do it," said Andy. "I'll just land on one foot."

"You will not be trying anything until your ankle has healed." Ellen's voice was firm. "We have a hard enough time keeping you healthy without getting doctors involved. No broken legs or torn ligaments."

Linnet took one look at her mother's face and knew better than to volunteer. Besides, the thought of landing on that foot almost made her sick.

"I'll do it," said Jake.

"Just one problem with that, kiddo," said Jan. "You don't have wings yet."

How could they be sure Jake would grow wings? wondered Linnet. "But what if—"

Ellen cut her off with a look, as if she knew precisely what was going on in Linnet's mind.

"What if what?" asked Jake.

"Uh," said Linnet, casting about for an idea. "What if, er, we just tried things on to see if they fit?"

"That's a great plan," Jan said. "It might even help you two cripples keep the weight off your bum legs."

"I'll get the equipment," said Charlie.

Ellen shook her head. "No. Those reporters could still be in the vicinity. Jake and I will take a walk later today to make sure they've gone. Until then, Sarah and I will have to do the grunt work."

"And me," said Jake, flexing his muscles.

"And Jake."

They went out. Linnet looked at the other three. Andy, with her great, dark wings, ought to be able to fly. Jan—well, it would take a lot of helium. Her wings were much smaller than Linnet's. And Charlie—if he ever flew, his twisted wings wouldn't have anything to do with it. She herself had the best chance.

Andy looked at Linnet, obviously thinking the same thing. "I am not going to let you fly all by yourself, you winged weirdo."

Linnet smiled. "Like anyone could stop you from flying."

Charlie went into the kitchen. He came out with a bemused expression on his face and a strange object in his hands, just as the others came in with the stuff.

Sarah buried her face in the pile of inflatable vests she was carrying. "Oh," she mumbled. "The bread."

"So that's what it is," said Charlie, holding up the flat brown stick.

Sarah flared up. "Well, what did you expect? These people come in and see this big pile of dough half made up, and I have to pretend that I'm making bread. You didn't even have a recipe."

"I don't use a recipe. I just know how to make it." He tapped the bread on the door frame.

"I hope you made the reporters eat some," said Jan.

Sarah smiled in spite of herself. "I tried," she said ruefully. "We couldn't even bite it."

"Why didn't you have Ellen help you?"

"I thought it would look strange for me to take over, since I'd just come in," said Ellen. She gave a huge smile. "Besides, I was having too much fun watching Sarah."

Charlie tapped harder.

"Let me do it," said Jake. He grabbed the loaf and swung. Whack. It hit the door frame and spun out of his fingers. "Ouch," he said.

"Door nothing; bread one," said Charlie, examining the frame. "One major dent."

Then they were all laughing, passing the indestructible bread around, tapping each other gently on the head. Andy got another loaf and fenced with Jake. "This is my dark saber," he yelled. "I'm Jake Skywalker."

Jan gave him a big hug. "Someday you really could be," she said.

That changed the focus, and suddenly they were getting Andy and Linnet carefully kitted out in various inflatables.

"I had to pretend I was throwing a big party and get some party balloons, too," said Ellen. "To throw off suspicion." She filled one with a ftttt—a brilliant fuchsia globe—tied the end, and let it float up to the ceiling.

"Do some more," cried Jake.

"Let me show you something first," said Charlie. He handed Ellen a purple balloon. "Fill this, please, but don't tie the end."

Ellen did as he asked, pinching the end tightly and handing it back to him. Charlie let the balloon deflate into his mouth. "Hello, boys and girls," he said in a comically high voice.

Jake yelped. "How did you do that?" Ellen released a blast of helium from another balloon in his face as he was speaking and "do that?" came out cartoony.

They all grabbed for balloons and filled them, breathing in the light gas and cracking up over their voices. "Okay," Jan squeaked. "For every balloon you breathe, you have to tie one. I want to have a party!"

Soon the living room was transformed, with orange and blue and green and every imaginable color bobbing up to the old open-beamed ceiling. Andy and Linnet were puffed up in yellow vests that left their backs free, with extra pouf around their necks and waist belts to hold them in place. Andy put a rainbow row of water wings up her arms and long legs. One red water wing escaped as Ellen was handing it to her and floated up to the ceiling.

"It's an omen," said Andy. "The water wings want to fly, and so do I."

She stepped back and, standing on one leg, began flapping furiously. The air currents sent balloons every which way.

It looked as if she was gaining a little height. Then one wing hit a floor lamp and knocked it over onto a coffee table. "Stop," yelled Ellen. "Wait until you can really try."

Jan picked up the lamp. "One scratched coffee table to add to the dented door frame."

"And my wrecked jeans," said Linnet.

"Not to mention knees and ankle," added her mother.

"If we only knew which tabloid to bill," said Ellen.

"They left a card somewhere," said Sarah. "I don't see it now, though."

"I'm so surprised," said Jan. "With the place so neat, a little scrap of paper should just stand out." She stirred through a puddle of flat balloons.

"It could be anywhere," said Andy. Did her voice sound odd, Linnet wondered, secretive? "It will probably turn up—someday." She stretched her wings to their full breadth.

But
you transform
all of it
into pure white wing,
white geometry,
the ecstatic line of your flight.

—*Pablo Neruda*, "Ode to the Seagull"

CHAPTER

Nineteen

Ellen kept the barn locked until Andy and Linnet were both healed to her satisfaction. While they were waiting, they spent a lot of time with binoculars, watching birds, trying to analyze how they flew. Hawks and eagles were the coolest and the easiest to watch, with their lazy spirals taking advantage of thermals. The little flitting birds were too fast to really understand. The book in Linnet's room, *Secrets of Animal Flight,* helped, but it was depressing, too, stating that humans would have to have wings much larger than theirs to fly.

Finally, Ellen unlocked the door. Then there were numerous glider flights to test the theory and application. It was working, Linnet thought, dropping lightly at the end of a run. She and Andy looked like a pair of Pillsbury

Doughboys who'd been in a paint fight, but they definitely had lift.

"We can fly," said Andy, landing behind her. "So let's fly."

Ellen shook her head. "We want to be careful. We'll do this for another day, and then we'll take the cable down and let you try it here, where the soft mats will catch you if there's a problem."

"Oh, come on," Linnet cried. Andy looked as if she were going to protest, too, but she said nothing.

After a couple more flights, Andy hissed, "Wait!" when Linnet was going to head back to the takeoff platform. "We're going to go get a snack, Ellen. Okay? Be right back."

She grabbed Linnet's arm and dragged her into the walkway. "I'm not going to wait," she whispered, breaking into a long-limbed run. "I'm going to fly right now. Want to watch?"

"Wait for me," said Linnet, running after her.

Andy was ahead all the way through the kitchen, but Linnet caught her when she turned to make the stairs. "We'll do it together," she said, grabbing one of Andy's wings.

"Hey, let go," said Andy, trying to flap. Linnet hung on. "Okay—together."

They went into Andy's room and opened the window.

Linnet scrambled out first, clumsy in her helium-filled paraphernalia. She gave Andy a hand out.

They stood on the roof together, a light breeze tugging at their wingtips. "Count of three?" said Andy, moving a step closer to the edge.

Linnet looked down at the ground and let her gaze move out, to the trees and mountains. "One."

Andy's voice joined hers. "Two."

They started flapping. "Three."

Linnet and Andy flew off the roof. Into the air. Out. Even up a little. Andy shrieked with joy. "Oh, Linnet!"

Linnet was too busy laughing to answer. This was what it was supposed to be like, having wings.

This time, she saw the tree coming well in advance, but she wasn't any better at turning. Maybe a little. She leaned to one side, lost her momentum, had to flap like crazy to avoid another crash landing. But she did. "Oh, Andy," she said, just as Andy took a dive into a clump of chokecherry bushes. Two of her water wings popped on impact.

"Wow," yelled Andy. "Did you see that?"

"I did," said Ellen's voice. She and Jan and Jake and Charlie were standing by the kitchen door with big grins on their faces. "Part of it anyway. Not in time to get the takeoff, though. Why didn't you let me get pictures?"

"Oh, we'll do it again," said Linnet. "Right, Andy?"

"When you're right, you're right. Except," she struggled out of the bushes, "I think we'll learn how to turn in the barn first."

Learning to turn was tricky. Finally, though, both were reasonably adept and comfortable launching off the roof outside their windows. For a while, Ellen or Sarah or Jake scouted the area on foot first, to dispel reporter paranoia, but they soon gave that up. Andy practically exploded one day when they wanted to fly and the wingless members of the group were busy doing other things and didn't want to reconnoiter just yet. "I am not going to be stuck in this house for the next eighty years," she screamed. "It's bad enough being up here in the middle of nowhere without being able to go outside until someone else says it's okay."

Ellen looked down at the aspen photograph she was mounting. Linnet thought she had tears in her eyes. "You're good for us, Andy," she said, after a silence. "Everyone else is too agreeable most of the time, too likely to do as they're told." She looked at Andy and Linnet in turn. "I think you're right; we can't shrink down the world even further. Use your own judgment on when to go outside and how far."

Andy stood there, trembling, until Linnet took her arm. "Come on. Let's go to the rocks."

They hadn't been there since the night the reporters

showed up. The possibility of someone watching—Linnet felt goose bumps spreading along her arms and wings as they walked through the dry late-summer grass. "What if they come back?" she asked.

Andy raised her chin. "Then they come back, and we get to be famous. Maybe we could be models." She struck a fashion pose. "I could be the next Charday. Or we could be rock stars."

"Except we can't play and can't sing," said Linnet.

"Speak for yourself," said Andy. She started singing an old Madonna song in some unknown key.

Linnet joined in. They sang all the way and then jumped up on the rocks and finished the performance, playing air guitar and flapping their wings.

"I can just see us on the Grammys, accepting the award for best band with wings," said Andy, sinking down into a sitting position.

"That's the only category we'd win." Linnet rubbed her ears and made a face.

"We just need more practice," said Andy, and started singing again. Linnet pretended to faint.

Okay, so they wouldn't end up as famous rock stars. But Linnet *could* see them on MTV, announcing songs or interviewing real rock stars. Maybe it wouldn't be so bad if the secret were revealed.

On the other hand, what would it be like to have reporters constantly circling around like sharks?

"Don't look so serious," said Andy, breaking into her thoughts.

Linnet let the day take over. The brilliant sky. The sun, warm on her wings. The dry ping of grasshoppers. A breeze sighing in the pines and spruces. She flared her wings to soak up the warmth. "I don't want summer to end," she said.

"It's really pretty up here in the fall," said Andy lazily. "The aspen trees turn bright yellow. It gets windier, too. That might help us fly."

"Maybe," said Linnet doubtfully, remembering the erratic winds of the storm.

Andy sat up straight. "Have you ever wondered how many other people have ever been here?"

"Huh?" Linnet didn't quite track the change in subject.

"Like Jake's father—was he a cutwing or what? And if he had wings, why isn't he still here?"

"Maybe we could ask—"

"Uh-uh," said Andy, shaking her head. "I started hinting around with Charlie once, to see if he knew. He said it was none of our business and if I was smart I wouldn't mention it to anyone—especially Jake."

None of them knew their fathers, Linnet thought. Except maybe Charlie, and how great could that have been?

Even her mother never said anything about a father. How long before Sarah's wings grew was Margaret left alone? It was amazing how many things Linnet did not know about her mother. And how reluctant she was to bring it up.

All of a sudden, she couldn't sit around on a rock, enduring this unreal life. "I've got to get back," she said, leaping down and taking off at a run on their faint path.

Sarah was in the garden, picking the green beans that the critters hadn't gotten to. Linnet slowed down, then made herself keep going.

She hadn't really spent much time with her mother since Sarah had come to the house. Almost anyone else was easier to talk to. But no one else knew whether Sarah had known her father or what it felt like to be Margaret's child. She scuffed her way into the garden and picked a couple of beans.

The garden became a bubble of tension around Linnet, and her mother clearly picked up on that. Linnet was afraid she'd take her bucket and go in. "What happened to your... to Margaret's husband?" she asked quickly.

Sarah's fingers stilled, but she kept looking at the bean plant in front of her. "He left," she said, her voice a whisper. "When I was too small to remember him."

"So he didn't know about your wings?"

"Unless Margaret told him later. I don't think she did, but"—she gave an uneasy laugh—"you know how it is in our family; we can't talk to our mothers."

Linnet felt her face go stiff. She didn't want to cry, but then she was.

"I'm sorry," said Sarah, coming close to her. She reached toward Linnet and let her hand drop without touching her. "It was supposed to be a joke."

It wasn't funny, Linnet thought. She had no future that made any kind of sense, and her only connection with her past was through this mother who wouldn't let there be a connection.

*Mr. and Mrs. Darling and Nana rushed into
the nursery too late. The birds were flown.*

—*J. M. Barrie*, Peter Pan

CHAPTER

Twenty

No connection—but that wasn't true. Linnet could talk to Margaret herself. The words Margaret had left her with sprang into her mind: "If you need me..."

The Livingston phone book was in the drawer beneath the phone. Linnet lurked around the kitchen waiting for it to be empty, but it never seemed to be. Finally, she volunteered to make biscuits.

"I'll help," said Andy.

"Can I cut them out?" asked Jake.

Just great. Linnet wiped the counter slowly. "I want to do it myself," she said.

"I never get to make biscuits," said Jake.

Jan looked at Linnet. "We'll make some on Saturday," she said. "This time it's Linnet's turn."

Andy simply flounced off, which was probably what she would have done if Linnet had demanded her help. Linnet sighed.

Making biscuits was no big deal, since they had big boxes of Bisquick. Charlie made everything from scratch, but the rest of them used mixes. Linnet measured out enough for a triple batch, which was the least amount that would feed them all. Finally, the area was clear.

She grabbed the phone book and looked up Margaret's number, feeling guilty.

No one was around right then, but Linnet couldn't bring herself to call. What if Ellen came through? What if her mother did? And she wasn't sure she wanted to talk to Margaret anyway. She stuffed the piece of paper with Margaret's phone number in her pocket and hurried through her excuse of a baking project.

The biscuits were bad. Linnet hadn't stirred them well enough before rolling them out, and there were gobs of dry powdery stuff. Andy make a point of dissecting hers carefully and inspecting each morsel before eating it. Jake threw a fit and had to leave the table for a few minutes. The adults had clearly made a silent pact not to say anything.

The atmosphere was as dry and miserable as the biscuits. Linnet felt as if everyone knew that she had Margaret's phone number in her pocket. Who knew what Andy's problem was; she didn't need much of an excuse to get into a snit. Maybe the little taste of freedom had backfired, reminding Andy that their full run of the place didn't mean much. Linnet bit into one of her awful biscuits; she'd taken a plateful just to prove that they were okay, and now she was determined to finish them.

Mistake. A puff of powder erupted in her mouth, and she somehow inhaled some into her lungs. She started coughing and choking. Charlie and Sarah both jumped up and acted as if they were about to try the Heimlich maneuver on her, but Linnet—still hacking, her eyes watering—waved them away. "I'll be fine," she managed to croak.

"I don't know if this will be a great favor," said Jan, gathering all the biscuits, including the ones from Linnet's plate, "but, with Linnet's permission, I'm going to feed these to the deer."

Linnet found herself giggling. "What if we have to use the Heimlich maneuver on a deer?"

"It would be hard enough to use it on Linnet," Ellen said, "without getting a black eye."

They all trooped out the kitchen door behind Jan and ceremoniously dumped the biscuits beside the feeding rock. "Caution," yelled Jake. "These biscuits are dangerous! Eat at your own risk."

When they were all back at the table, eating crackers

with their soup instead of biscuits, Jan made a toast. "To the health of the deer."

They raised their glasses, and Charlie added, "And to a safe home."

Linnet saw Andy stiffen beside her, felt the same stiffness herself. Tension. Anticipation. Fear and excitement.

Andy said, "Safe. Boring." She set her glass down. "I can't drink to that one. I'm sick of this place."

Ellen flushed. "It hasn't been easy—"

"I know, I know," said Andy. "But it isn't easy thinking of living here forever either, like I'm in prison or something."

"This is a sanctuary," Charlie said promptly. "A safe place, the only one I can even imagine."

Andy let out a snort.

"I've believed that all along," Ellen said slowly. "This is a place where we can keep our secret without *anyone* interfering. Without anyone thinking they know better—"

"Like who's to know?" Andy said sarcastically.

Ellen took a breath and looked around. "No one," she said. "I just meant—this is *our* place, a place where we can live in peace."

"Big deal," Andy muttered.

"It is a big deal," said Charlie. "If I'd had a place like this when I was younger, I wouldn't have wings like this." He stretched them to their terrible, wasted limit. "My parents wouldn't have bound my wings to try to keep them from growing. They wouldn't have kept me locked in the basement when that didn't work. They wouldn't have beat..."

His voice failed, dropped into the utter stillness. No one could speak to that story. Linnet shut her eyes, wishing she could turn off the pictures in her mind.

After a few long minutes, Charlie whispered, "So it is important."

"Or if it wasn't a secret at all," countered Andy. "If everyone knew, then no one would have to hide it. Anywhere."

"If everyone knew," said Jan, "we wouldn't have to hide. That's true. But we wouldn't be able to hide either. Do you think it would be easy to be a winged person in a normal world?"

"Do you think it's easy to be a winged person without a world?" said Andy.

"My mother has created a place—" Jan began hotly.

Ellen cut her off. "I want to hear the opinion of all of the winged and those who will be winged. Jake and Andy and Linnet have their whole lives to live with wings—they have as much or more to say about this as any of us."

Jan and Charlie exchanged glances. "But they don't always think long term," said Charlie. "Maybe they never do. Maybe they can't. How can they—how can any of us—know what it would be like to have people staring at us all the time? We need this sanctuary."

"So keep it," said Andy. "We'll go somewhere else." She looked at Sarah, who was sitting absolutely still and absolutely silent. "Linnet's mom can take us somewhere else."

Linnet felt cold. All those eyes. What would it be like? Could she stand it?

"What do you think, Linnet?" Ellen asked. "And you, Jake?"

"I say what my mom says," said Jake.

Linnet felt everyone's eyes on her. And this was nothing compared to what the real world would be like. Maybe Andy could take it, but... "I don't know," she began, then stopped.

Andy read her answer before Linnet could make herself finish. "You are all cowards," she said, shoving her chair back so hard that it fell over. She didn't even look at Linnet as she stalked away, her eyes bright with tears.

When the door to Andy's room slammed above Linnet's head, the vibration cut through the center of her. Andy would never forgive her for this. No more moonlight excursions. No more sessions out at the rocks. No more joking or flying together. No more stupid fights even. Andy would never speak to her again.

"I'll do the dishes," said Ellen, gathering them almost violently. "Now it's *my* turn to be alone in the kitchen."

They all dispersed, slowly. For a moment it seemed that Sarah might be about to say something to Linnet, but then she turned and went into the living room.

Ellen looked at Linnet over an armful of soup bowls. "Not exactly the evening we wanted to have," she said softly.

Linnet's fear escaped into words. "Andy will never talk to me again."

This time it was Ellen who didn't say anything, and Linnet read her answer from the expression on her face: *very likely not.* Linnet ran for her own room.

It was dark when Linnet woke on her damp pillow: 1:27 A.M. She had dreamed that her window was open and people were looking in at her. Or maybe just one person. Someone angry and hurt, who looked like Andy but with no wings.

The dream was so real that Linnet got up and peeked behind her shade to make sure the window was shut and latched. It might as well have been open, though; she couldn't get back to sleep.

Falling asleep again in the middle of the night was much harder now than it had been without wings. There was really only one comfortable position—lying on her stomach—that worked, so she couldn't shift around. She'd been trying, though, for close to an hour, when a disturbing thought made her sit up straight. What if it had been Andy's window opening that had wakened her?

Linnet crept out of bed and made her way into Andy's room, as silent as a deer. Even before she turned on the light, she could see that her fear was a reality: the window was open, and Andy was gone.

CHAPTER

Twenty-one

With the light on, Linnet found a note on Andy's nightstand: "Off to see the world. Don't be surprised if you see me on the news." There was no signature, but one wasn't necessary. Linnet sat on Andy's bed to think.

It was her fault that Andy had gone, alone in the night. If she had been braver, they could have all gone together, Sarah and Linnet and Andy. She shivered in the chill night air coming through the open window. Andy would freeze out there. Maybe she'd taken the emergency blanket from Ellen's Jeep.

A few seconds later, Linnet was pulling her jeans on. She hesitated and put the plastic letter opener she'd taken from the motel in her pocket, skeptical that it would be of much use, but somehow feeling safer anyway. She would just check the Jeep and see if the blanket was gone. That was all. *It won't take long,* she told herself, as she went back to Andy's room and out the open window.

The blanket was still in the coffee can in the Jeep. Linnet stood there, crinkling the thin, silvery material in her fingers. If Andy was out there in the night, she needed this.

But could Linnet find her? In the entire wilderness? Even as she was thinking this, Linnet was going through the rest of the items in the can. Matches. She took them out of the glass jar and stuck them in her pocket. The flashlight. The old candy bars. Skip the plastic water.

Linnet closed the Jeep door as quietly as she could and stood in the darkness. Maybe this was simpler than she'd thought at first. Andy was headed for the real world. That meant there was only one way she could have gone: the driveway and then the road. "I'll just take her the blanket," she whispered to herself.

Walking alone along the driveway was even worse than the trip back to the house the night the reporters came, even though Linnet had a working flashlight this time. For a while, she tried not to use it, because it made her feel so visible. That was stupid, she decided; the only other person likely to be out here was Andy, and she wanted to be visible to Andy.

She tried not to think of what her chances were of finding the older girl, with her longer stride and head start.

With the emergency blanket draped over her wings like a shawl, reflecting her own heat back toward her, Linnet was fairly warm. The circle of light kept her from tripping on rocks. After a while, the tension between her wings relaxed. "Andy," she called every few minutes. "Andieeeee."

When she got to the road, Linnet stopped. The house was behind her, and the others and her warm bed. Somewhere ahead, cold and alone, was Andy. She fingered the edge of the blanket. She'd just go a little farther. If she didn't find Andy soon, she'd turn back.

Just a little farther. Just a little farther. Just a little farther. "Annddieeeeee."

There was a quiet answer from behind a tree. "I could have scared you to death just now."

"Andy!"

Andy stepped into the circle of Linnet's light. "You're blinding me," she said.

"Sorry," said Linnet, pointing at Andy's feet instead of her face.

"What are you doing here?" Andy asked. There was no expression in her voice.

"I, uh, brought you a blanket," said Linnet. "I thought you'd be cold."

There was a click and Andy's light came on, dim and weak, revealing her own shoulders, draped in red-and-black-striped wool. "I have one," she said. "From my bed." She clicked her light off again.

"Oh . . ." Linnet's voice trailed off.

"Shut off your flashlight," Andy said. "It's bad enough that *my* batteries are dying."

Linnet did as she was commanded, and they were alone in the dark. "I'm sorry," she said.

"Are you?"

The cool voice from the darkness infuriated Linnet. "What do you want?" she yelled. "Just because I don't want to be a freak—"

"Well, you are one," said Andy. "And I am, too. And so are Jan and Charlie, and Jake's probably going to be one. We're all freaks until having wings is just one more normal way to be, like having red hair or brown eyes."

"And how long is that going to take?" Linnet asked sarcastically. "Until we have grandchildren?"

"Maybe." Andy's voice shook with tears. "Maybe. I just know that it's never going to happen unless somebody takes the risk."

Linnet could not deny that. All her arguments died inside her. "But why does it have to be us?" she whispered.

"Because I'm such a pain in the butt," Andy said, half laughing, half sobbing. "And you're my friend."

"Let's go back to the house," said Linnet. "I'll tell them tomorrow we're going to try it."

Somewhere nearby they heard the sound of an engine. "We'd better get off the road," said Linnet. "If someone sees us here, the place won't be secret for the others."

They plunged off the road into the darkness, using intermittent splashes of Andy's weak light. "Just like old times," Andy whispered, as they crouched behind a gnarled cedar to let the car pass. "WINGED WEIRDOS ROAM AGAIN."

They continued through the night, roughly following the road, heading back toward the house. Andy's flashlight died, and she stuck it in her belt bag. By comparison, the beam from Linnet's light was so bright they felt conspicuous, so they moved farther from the road. "I almost wish the batteries would die down a little," Linnet said, partially shielding the lens with her fingers.

"Don't say that—it might happen."

And then it did.

It was far from dawn, according to their best guess, when Linnet's flashlight ghosted into nothing.

Andy swore quietly. "Now what are we going to do?"

Linnet tried to dredge up some courage by repeating back Andy's suggestions from the last time they were stuck in the dark. "The usual. Fall over a cliff. Get eaten by rabid termites. Scream. Or maybe follow the stream back to the house."

Andy's laugh was hollow. "The last one's the best—except there's no stream."

"It's got to be here somewhere," said Linnet. She took one cautious step, stopped before she could take another. "Are there rattlesnakes out at night?"

"No."

Linnet felt an extreme lack of relief in the short answer and the tone of voice in which Andy had delivered it. It took her a moment to figure out the reason: snakes were about the only thing she didn't want to see that wouldn't be out at night. Bears, coyotes, wolves from Yellowstone Park. Ellen had even heard rumors of a mountain lion in the area. Jan wouldn't let Jake go outside by himself, but Linnet thought the fact that there were two of them here now would mean nothing more to any mountain lion than the chance for a bigger midnight snack.

They blundered on for a few steps, and then Andy pulled back. "How do we know we're going the right direction?"

"We'll just go the same way the road goes—"

"If I knew where the road was, I'd walk down the middle of it," said Andy roughly.

"You don't know where the road is?" Linnet's throat closed up, and her words came out as a squeak.

"Well, do you?"

"But I thought..."

"I thought we were heading in the direction of the house," said Andy. Her voice faltered. "But now all the directions seem the same: wrong."

Falling over a cliff became more of a possibility. "Maybe we really should scream," Linnet said.

"That might attract animals."

"Like bears?"

"Or wolves. Or mountain lions."

They spent a couple of minutes trying to figure out which animal they most wanted not to attract. They settled on mountain lions, although none of them sounded great. Even a skunk would be awful.

"It's too bad we can't start a fire," said Andy, sitting down. "I didn't bring matches."

"Matches!" Linnet shrieked. "Oh, Andy, you're wonderful."

"I said I *didn't* bring matches."

"But I did," said Linnet. "And you just reminded me." She dug into the right front pocket of her jeans. Something warm and gooey met her fingers.

In what distant deeps or skies,
Burnt the fire of thine eyes?
On what wings dare he aspire?
What the hand dare sieze the fire?

— *William Blake*, "The Tyger"

CHAPTER

Twenty-two

Linnet withdrew her hand quickly. "Eww." In the darkness, she couldn't see what covered her fingers.

"What's the matter?" asked Andy.

Linnet cautiously brought her hand near her face and sniffed. Chocolate. She groaned. The candy bars.

"What?" Andy's voice was more demanding now.

"I had some candy from the emergency kit in my pocket, and it melted. The wrapper must have bro—"

"The same pocket as the matches?" A note of accusation.

"Well, at least I brought matches."

"Yum, my favorite—chocolate-covered matches."

The only responses Linnet could think of would just make Andy madder. She lowered herself to the ground and silently licked the stale, melted chocolate from her fingers.

"I shouldn't be near you," said Andy, standing up.

"Why?"

"Because bears love chocolate," she said.

"Oh, thanks for pointing that out."

Silence from Andy for a moment. When she did speak, her voice was unexpectedly contrite. "I'm sorry; that was mean."

Another silence. Linnet tried to accept the apology, couldn't come up with a gracious reply. "Do you really think bears will come?" she asked instead.

"I doubt it," said Andy.

Unless they smell winged weirdos and chocolate-covered matches, thought Linnet miserably.

They spent the rest of the night next to a pine tree, huddled in their blankets, too keyed up to sleep. Linnet kept imagining that she heard hungry predators crackling the underbrush nearby, but she couldn't say anything to Andy for fear of attracting unwanted attention. *Probably just chipmunks,* she kept telling herself, but she was unconvinced.

A long night, the longest she'd ever spent. And one of the coldest. A person had to be radiating body heat for the emergency blanket to reflect it back, and Linnet decided she wasn't doing much radiating after a while.

Eventually, despite the cold and fear and uncomfortable position, Linnet fell asleep.

In the clear cold morning, something nudged her awake. Something warm. Linnet opened her eyes to find a bear nosing at her pocket.

Linnet screamed. She scooted sideways into a groggy Andy, who added her own scream. The bear backed away with a scared bawl and ran. Linnet and Andy ran the other way, their blankets catching on bushes.

"It wasn't a very big bear," Andy wheezed, when they couldn't run any farther.

Linnet crouched down, turning her head from side to side as she caught her breath. "I don't care," she said. "It was a bear and it was trying to get in my pocket."

They fell to the ground then, laughing hysterically at the image of a bear in Linnet's pocket. The wild laughter mixed with sobs of fear and relief.

Linnet wiped her eyes and looked around. "I have no idea where we are," she said.

Andy stood up and turned. "Neither do I. But I think we just have to go west. Unless—" Her voice broke off.

"Unless what?"

"Unless we've already gone too far north."

They didn't have a clue.

"We should pick a direction and keep going," said Andy.

"Aren't you supposed to stay put when you're lost?" Linnet asked.

"Aren't you the one with the chocolate pocket? There's a bear around here, in case you forgot."

"But maybe it's just visiting. Maybe it lives in whatever direction we might go."

There was no right decision, it seemed. They argued for a while, and then they went a little way west and then a little way south. None of the ridges or trees or outcroppings of rock looked familiar.

"I'm starving," said Linnet. She scraped a little chocolate out of her pocket and licked it off her fingers.

"I'm starving and thirsty."

Thirsty. It would be so nice to find a stream. You weren't supposed to drink out of streams and rivers, because you could get backpacker's diarrhea, but right then Linnet would have taken her chances.

Andy rubbed the back of her hand across her face. "We're never going to find our way back."

"Then they'll send someone to look for us," said Linnet. "A search party. Park rangers."

"Will they?" Andy looked skeptical. "And what would they say? Look for two lost girls and, oh, they just happen to have wings."

Linnet swallowed her assurance. When Andy put it that way, it seemed impossible. "But anyway, Ellen and Jake and my mom will look for us."

"In the wrong place," said Andy. "Probably around the rocks." Her expression brightened. "My note, though. That ought to tell them we went to the road."

"Uh..." Linnet didn't want to tell her that the note was in the same pocket as the melted candy and the ruined matches.

"What?"

"I—uh, the note..."

Andy gave her a look. "Just say it, whatever it is."

"I took the note with me."

"Oh, great," said Andy. "Brilliant."

"Well, you've been real brilliant about this whole thing, too," said Linnet. "Not bringing any food or matches or water."

"*I,*" said Andy, "was going to walk along the road and catch a ride to civilization with someone. I brought money."

"You were going to hitchhike?" asked Linnet. "Do you know how dangerous that is? That's really stupid."

"I don't know that it's any more dangerous than luring bears to your pocket with melted chocolate," said Andy.

A different thought struck Linnet. "It's a good thing I did take your note," she said with satisfaction, sitting on a rock to rest. "Otherwise, they'd think we were hitchhiking along the road, and they'd look for us there. We're probably closer to the rocks than we are to the road."

"We're probably closer to the bear than we are to either," Andy muttered.

After several minutes of hostile silence, Linnet buried her head in her knees. "What are we going to do?"

"Too bad we can't just fly up in the air and find the house."

"Up!" said Linnet. "We should climb up somewhere high. Maybe we'll see something we recognize."

"When you're right, you're right," said Andy with a grin.

It amazed Linnet how quickly Andy could go from angry to amiable, but it was something she had learned not to mention. They tied their blankets around their waists and set off together for a high ridge just to the west.

Nothing was sprained. That was the only good thing about their hungry, thirsty, tired trek up the ridge. It was steeper than it looked, with untrustworthy vegetation apt to uproot. Linnet found herself unable to judge whether rocks were firmly embedded or ready to roll. She herself almost rolled a couple of times, stopped once by a desperate grab at a thorny wild rose and another time by flopping forward against the rocky ground. Andy was in similar straits. At least their wings were a big help with balance, since there wasn't a wind. Linnet shuddered to think what it would be like to climb this in a stiff breeze.

They were about halfway up when it occurred to Linnet that a ridge was the worst place to be when you were hoping to happen upon a stream. Instantly, her thirst increased.

Maybe they'd see one below, though. And have to make a precarious, slipping trip down. Linnet shook her head and tested the rock above her for stability. It was stupid to be worrying about the dangers of descending to a stream that might not even be there when they weren't at the top yet.

Not surprisingly, long-legged Andy reached the top first, even with the bulky wool blanket slowing her down. "Just great," Linnet heard her mutter, as she made her way up the last few yards.

Nothing looked familiar. And yet it all did. Neither girl, raised in town, had developed the habit of analyzing terrain and landmarks. And there were no streams visible either.

"Now what?" said Andy.

"Maybe we should stay here a little while," said Linnet, collapsing against a rock and panting. "If someone is looking for us, they might see us better up here. Or we might see them."

"I'm not too anxious to go anywhere right now anyway," said Andy. She made herself comfortable. "At least if we have to be lost, it's pretty out right now."

Linnet nodded. A few of the aspens had begun to turn golden. Having just climbed to the top of a ridge, though, she noticed a new, harsh aspect to the scenery. What it must have been like to be a pioneer, before roads and cars, trekking across the plains and mountains in a covered wagon. Try as she might, she couldn't place herself there.

Even in her mind, the idea of a girl with wings in a covered wagon was too strange.

And what about other times? Maybe people with wings were responsible for some of the ancient Greek myths. Or rumors of fairies in Ireland and England. Although if winged people had been around that long, surely there'd be proof by now. Surely, with all her reading she would have found concrete evidence of them.

"Do you think we're some new thing?" she asked Andy. "I mean, why haven't we heard of people with wings?"

"Maybe it's some weird genetic mutation," said Andy. She had spread the wool blanket on the ground and was stretched out. "Maybe the effects of pollution or atomic bomb testing or something. You know, like those three-legged frogs."

Exactly what Linnet had been thinking before. But wouldn't there be lots more winged people if that were the case? Before Linnet could comment, she heard a low thwapping sound. "Listen," she said.

Andy sat up and they both looked around. "A helicopter," she said. "They've got a helicopter looking for us."

"There," said Linnet, pointing it out, an odd speck, rapidly growing.

The helicopter made a zigzag pattern, coming closer and closer. They stood up and waved and yelled and flapped their wings.

The pilot was clearly looking more seriously at the lower ground, but there was no time to climb down now. All they could do was what they were doing, but more so. Linnet felt herself getting hoarse, which was stupid, because she bet the helicopter was so loud inside that the crew could barely hear themselves. But she kept yelling anyway.

The chopper was almost level with them and not so far away when the pilot looked across and saw them. A startled expression hit his face, which wasn't a surprise, Linnet thought, given the strange sight of two girls with wings leaping about on a ridge in the mountains.

*The long, long wings curled up like the last glimmering slice
of an almost new moon, and then Daedelus came into view—
gigantic wings, but so thin that they almost vanished in the
sparkling sun—and passed over their heads.*

—*Gary Dorsey,* The Fullness of Wings:
The Making of a New Daedalus

CHAPTER

Twenty-three

Andy waved the red blanket. "Tie that on," Linnet shouted, as the helicopter approached, "or it might blow away."

Andy complied instantly while Linnet waved her hands. The helicopter hovered not far off, and the pilot gestured that they were to duck down.

They crouched, arms shielding their faces from the stinging wind, wings folded tightly, as the helicopter landed on a bare, rocky area nearby. The pilot flipped a door open and signaled for them to come.

They looked at each other, uncertain for a moment. Should they trust him? "So much for the dangers of hitchhiking," Andy yelled as they made their way through the manufactured wind, wings furled as tightly as possible.

The wind—if not the noise—decreased as soon as they

were inside. "Buckle in," the man yelled, reaching over to shut the door. He didn't seem surprised by the fact that they had wings. He moved a stick, and the helicopter rose into the sky at an angle.

Linnet wondered whether they'd made a huge mistake, but there was nothing she could do about it now, short of leaping from the helicopter and trusting her wings. Andy looked as nervous as she felt.

The helicopter banked and headed for a small clearing. As soon as they touched down, the pilot cut the engine and turned toward them.

They shrank back. "Don't be afraid," he said. "We don't have a lot of time." He seemed to notice how that sounded and gave an impatient smile. "We don't want to draw attention to the ranch. I'll drop you off nearby, and you can walk home after I leave. Have someone call after I've gone and report that you've come home."

"But—" Linnet started, unsure of how to say this.

"You're wondering why I'm not surprised about your wings," he said.

"Exactly," Andy said.

He started to unbutton his shirt, and they drew back even farther. Linnet reached in her pocket for the letter opener and held it menacingly, even though it was covered with chocolate.

"Sorry," he said, stopping, raising his hands. "That was

stupid. I was just going to show you my back. I used to have wings."

"What!" they both said together.

"There are quite a few of us who are pilots," he said. He tried to smile, but it didn't quite come off. "Our way of flying."

"Quite a few of us?" asked Andy. "You know more people with wings?"

"There are more of us who used to have wings and don't anymore," he said, his face grim. "But, yes, I know people with wings. All over the country. And in other countries as well."

He fumbled in his pocket and handed Andy a card with a phone number on it. "This will get you in contact with the network. If you need travel arrangements or emergency medical care..."

Linnet just sat there, stunned, as Andy accepted the card. Mechanically, she put the letter opener back in her pocket.

"Or you can try the Web site—WingNet.com."

Linnet sputtered, "But that said *myths* about wings."

"I know—it's not perfect—trying to keep a secret and still get the information out." He looked at his watch. "We have to get going. When I stop close to the house, you need to get out as quickly as possible and hide until you see me leave. I won't really land, just sort of hover near the ground. Give you a chance to try out those wings."

The rotors started, slowly at first, and then became a circular blur. The helicopter lifted straight up and entered the valley, flying near the treetops.

If she hadn't been so dazed by the whole wing network thing, Linnet would probably have been scared, but nothing seemed real now. They dipped and rose, skimming over the trees, blurs of green and darker green and yellow. There was a stream not far—as the helicopter flies—from where they'd been, but her thirst had left her as well.

There were others. They could travel.

The pilot interrupted her thoughts. "I'll set you down here," he yelled. "Can you find your way home?"

Linnet looked down at the familiar rocks. She looked at Andy, and they burst out laughing, nodding idiotically. The pilot laughed. "Bye, bye birdies," he said, lowering the chopper slowly.

Andy opened the door. "Thanks," she yelled. She perched in the doorway, hesitated.

"Go on," the pilot yelled.

Linnet gave her a gentle push, and Andy fell, flapping automatically, to land safely, if awkwardly.

"Your turn," the pilot said.

"Thank you." It felt weird to have her words swallowed up by the overwhelming sound. Linnet dangled her legs out.

"See you later," he yelled.

Linnet jumped, poising her wings. It was almost impossible to fly in the helicopter's wind, but she didn't have far to go, and she managed to land.

The helicopter rose a few yards, and the pilot waved. Linnet and Andy headed for home, waving as they ran, their wings catching the wind, pushing them along.

"I can't believe this," said Andy, her eyes sparkling. "Can you?"

Linnet shook her head. There was something bothering her about the whole thing, but she couldn't think about it and keep up with Andy at the same time.

Andy pulled ahead, and then she turned, dancing around. "Hurry up, slowpoke."

Linnet caught up and they ran to the house, more or less together, in a twisting path that avoided—barely—trees and rocks and most of the bushes.

They hit the kitchen door at the same time and had to disentangle wings and take turns. For a wonder, Linnet made it in first.

"We're back," she called. "We're back. And guess what!" Even as she said it, she figured out what was bothering her: someone in the house had to know already, because otherwise the network wouldn't have sent a helicopter to find them.

Of course in the end Wendy let them fly away together. Our last glimpse of her shows her at the window, watching them receding into the sky until they were as small as stars.

—*J. M. Barrie*, Peter Pan

CHAPTER

Twenty-four

The others crowded into the kitchen in a bunch, with Jake in the lead. "You guys are in trouble!" he said.

"Where have you been?" asked Ellen. She looked terrible; they all did. Including, Linnet realized, Andy and almost certainly herself. The drained expression on her mother's face made Linnet feel worse, made her think about the time when she first came to the ranch and Sarah hadn't known where she was. As bad as it had been for Linnet herself, not knowing where her mother was for those weeks, it must have been worse for Sarah. And then to think of Margaret, who had wondered for thirteen years about her missing daughter, feeling blame and dread.

"I have to have a drink of water," she said, grabbing glasses from the cupboard, handing one to Andy.

"Linnet!" said Sarah, her voice sharp. "Where were you? We were so worried."

"I just went to get Andy, and we got lost—"

"Never mind about that," Andy interrupted. "That's not the important part." She pulled a business card triumphantly from her pocket and handed it to Ellen.

"You've been talking to those reporters?" Ellen sounded surprised, angry, and disbelieving.

Andy grabbed the card back. "Sorry, wrong card." She fished in her pocket again and gave Ellen a second card.

"What is it?" asked Jan.

"A phone number," Ellen said dryly. "What's going on?"

"It's a network—" Andy began.

"Across the country," added Linnet.

"The pilot was one," Andy said.

Ellen sat down. "Oh," she said. "He told you."

"What are you talking about?" demanded Jan.

"We got lost and we got rescued," said Linnet. "And the pilot—"

"The pilot," said Andy, "was a cutwing."

Stunned gasps from everyone except Ellen.

"That's the number for a network of people with wings and cutwings, and we can call if we want to travel or if we get sick."

Jan wavered, caught the back of a chair. "I think I'd better sit down," she said. "A network? Really?"

"This is an incredible coincidence," Charlie said, sitting himself.

Ellen bit her lip. She seemed much older all of a sudden. "It's not a coincidence."

"What do you mean?" Andy asked.

"The network," said Ellen. "I've known since—for a long time. I called them when the girls were missing."

Jan's eyes narrowed, and her cheeks looked hot. "You've known and you didn't tell us?"

"I had my reasons."

Silence then.

So it was Ellen. Thinking back, Linnet could remember some clues. But did it even matter? She took a drink. It tasted as good as anything she'd ever had in her life. She was safe. The world had expanded. She had a future. She gulped her water too fast.

"I wonder," Charlie said, after Linnet's coughing had subsided, "if the others have figured out how to do the Heimlich maneuver on someone with wings."

"I'm sure they have," said Ellen mechanically. "They were always big on scientific tests. They probably know everything."

There was a harshness to her voice, a story behind it they didn't know yet. Jan ignored that. "We have the right to know. All these years here—knowing only a few other people. How could you?"

"I told you; I had my reasons."

"They'd better be good ones." Linnet had never heard Jan sound so angry.

"I don't want—"

Jan interrupted her mother. "I don't care whether you want to tell us or not."

"Very well," said Ellen. She seemed to be talking only to Jan. "I've known about the network since before you were born. I used to be a part of it. But just because people have wings—or used to have wings—doesn't mean they have good ideas. All it takes is one misguided person with power..." Her voice trailed off.

Charlie's voice broke the silence. "But if it were a case of one person, other people's ideas could take over. One person doesn't last forever. Look at Nazi Germany."

"Look at Iraq and how long Saddam Hussein's ideas—" Andy began.

"We're not talking Saddam Hussein and Hitler here," Ellen said. "It wasn't really that bad." She rubbed her eyes. "Let's say that I had disagreements with the leadership. Maybe I was wrong; he—they certainly were. But maybe not so wrong we couldn't have worked it out." She looked at Jan, at the others. "I'm sorry. I should have told you. There just never seemed to be a good way."

"Why not?" asked Jan.

"Because the person whom I had the disagreements with was your father."

A dead silence filled the room.

Jan let her breath out slowly. "We will talk about this later. In private."

"Yes," said Ellen.

"Oh, come on," said Andy. "This is more than just some bad divorce thing. We're talking about our future."

"You're right," said Ellen, sounding tired. "Okay. Now that you all know, there are definite benefits to be had by taking advantage of the network's resources. It is possible for people with wings to move around and still be hidden from the rest of the world."

"I can't believe it." Charlie looked as if he might cry at any second.

Jan opened her mouth, looked at Jake, closed it again. She was still mad, Linnet thought. It would be too bad if their discovery of the network messed things up between Jan and Ellen.

"So where do we go first?" asked Andy. "Paris? Hawaii? I'd love to go to a beach somewhere."

"Well, unless the network owns an island—which is possible—I doubt that a beach is going to be an option," said Ellen. "There are new possibilities, but they don't cover everything."

Something deflated within Linnet. "It's still the same," she said.

"Huh?" Andy looked at her.

"'Welcome to the teeny tiny world of the winged,'"

Linnet said. "Remember when you said that to me? It's still the same. Bigger now, but it's not the whole world."

"You can't live in the whole world at once anyway," said Jan.

Andy broke in. "But you should be able to decide where and when to go. I'm with Linnet. This secret network doesn't really change things. It's like saying as long as the slaves can go north, they don't need to be free in the South."

"And since it's a *secret* network and not everyone knows about it, things can still happen, like they did to Charlie and Ellen and my mother and Margaret," said Linnet. "Because it's still a secret."

Faced with these two thoughts, the room sobered. Charlie turned away.

"Well?" said Ellen, looking at them each in turn.

Jan sighed. "She's right. We'd just be hiding in a bigger room. It isn't real freedom." She hugged Jake. "I guess we need to expand our choices—like maybe get these kids to college."

"Or grade school?" asked Jake. Laughter sputtered around the room, went out.

Sarah looked at her hands. "I guess so. But since I don't have wings anymore, I don't think I should say."

"Charlie?" Ellen's voice was firm and compassionate.

It was a long time before Charlie whispered, "I don't

want to live in the whole world." His twisted wings shook. "But I don't want this to happen to other people."

"So we need this sanctuary still. Agreed?"

Nods all around.

"Are we back to Andy's original plan, then? For Sarah to take the girls somewhere else and then go public?"

Charlie turned back, facing the group once again. Linnet and Andy looked at each other.

"I don't want to go," Sarah said suddenly.

"Why?" asked Ellen.

"I just don't," Sarah cried.

"We can't let Andy and Linnet go alone."

A deep anger flared within Linnet. She couldn't count on her mother. She looked over at Sarah, about to lash out, and saw her mother exchanging glances with Charlie. Her mother and Charlie? Even as she was thinking it wasn't possible, her mind was doing the math: only two or three years' difference in age. The anger died inside her, replaced with wonder and confusion.

A look of comprehension bloomed on Andy's face. "We'll go with someone else then," she said.

"Who?" asked Ellen. "I have my work here. I can't take you. And there's no one else without wings."

"Margaret," said Linnet. "My grandmother. She said if I ever needed anything..." She felt guilty saying it, after what had happened to her mother. Sarah closed her eyes for a second and then gave Linnet a wispy smile and a nod.

"You'd need a van," said Ellen. "The secret wouldn't last for a mile in Margaret's car. Or Sarah's."

"We can call the network number," said Andy. "Maybe they'd send us a helicopter."

"More likely they'd say to rent a van," said Jan, ever practical.

"We still might be better off doing this on our own," said Ellen, "without involving the network at all."

"I don't buy that," said Jan. "And if it's true, that's all the more reason to get involved and change things. Think how much better it would be for a big group of people to reveal their wings rather than two young girls and a cut-wing grandmother."

Ellen hesitated. "Perhaps you have a point. And it wouldn't hurt for the girls to try their wings in a bigger room before they take on the whole world. But they should still have someone they know with them."

"We'll have to call Mar—" Sarah stopped, started again. "We'll have to call my mother, see if she's willing."

Grown-up planning stuff. Linnet looked at Andy again, scratched and dirty and tired—and ready to take on the world. "I get the shower first," Linnet said, darting for the stairs.

Of course, Andy won.

It doesn't matter, Linnet thought, leaning against the

wall in the hallway, waiting. The possibilities in her mind refreshed her more than any shower could. Other kids with wings. People who had experimented with different flying techniques. And beyond that, at some point, being able to walk down any street in any town and—

Linnet gave a determined smile. Why walk? With the whole world watching, she was going to fly.

*   *   *

Quick! A Sharper rustling!
And this linnet flew!

—*Emily Dickinson*